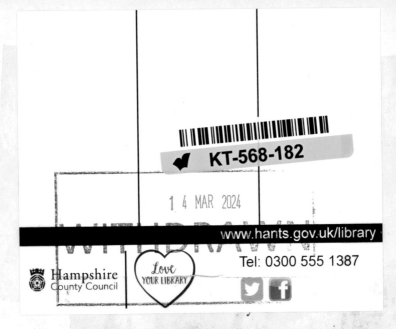

www.wyckerton.com

Publisher: Matador
9 Priory Business Park
Wistow Road, Kibworth Beauchamp,
Leicestershire, LE8 0RX
Tel: 0116 279 2299
Fax: 0116 297 2277
Email: books@troubador.co.uk
Web: www.troubadour.co.uk/matador

2nd EDITION
ISBN 978 1780885 735

www.wyckerton.com

British Library Cataloging in Publication Data.
A catalogue record for this book is available from the British Library.

Matador is an imprint of Troubedor Publishing Ltd

Printed and Bound by CPI Group (UK) Ltd, Croydon, CR0 4YY

For
Tim, who read the first draft.
Andy and Kate, who listened.
Barbara, who was indispensible.
And
Michael,
My Inspiration.

CONTENTS

CONTENTS

Read on
to discover
what this story
entails,
But bear in mind
it began
with an old
wives' tale...

"Friday night's dream, On the Saturday told,
Is sure to come true, Be it never too old."

CHAPTER ONE

Inklings

EVERY night Alfie watched the lights from the city of Wyckerton through his bedroom window. It glowed in the distance surrounded by its city wall. The moonlight flowed through the clouds then separated. The scattered light lit the city and made it appear mysterious. During the day nothing suggested that Wyckerton was anything but normal, yet at night Alfie felt the city was forbidden. *Why have I never been allowed to stay after dark?* As he stared, something deep inside him told him that it wasn't an ordinary city. It was special.

He could see those strange birds again. They weren't there every night. They climbed and swooped over Wyckerton. He'd accepted them as part of the city's strangeness. He never saw them during the day. *Where do they come from?*

'Derek, look. Those weird birds are back,' said Alfie.

Derek, his best friend, lay on the spare bed. He sighed then moved slowly over to the window.

'They don't look weird to me,' Derek said and returned to the bed.

'What? There's no way they're normal. Look at them.'

'I did and they look fine.' Derek sounded bored.

Alfie huffed. 'You can't be serious. Surely you can see they're strange.'

'Maybe they're slightly odd. Why does it matter?'

'Because…' Alfie couldn't think of a good reason. He squashed his nose onto the glass. He was glad that it was the school holiday so that he could stay up watching them as they swooped over Wyckerton.

During the holiday Alfie's father allowed Derek to stay over any night of the week. They made a pact never to talk about school. They pretended it didn't exist. Alfie worried that the days were passing too quickly. They only had a couple of weeks of freedom left. He didn't want to be the first to admit that starting senior school was scary.

Alfie's bedroom door opened. His father came into the room.

'It's late, boys. Get ready for bed, please.'

'Five more minutes?' asked Alfie, without turning away from the window.

'That's all though. I'm going to bed now. Goodnight.' He closed the door as he left.

Alfie's father let them choose when to go to sleep. He usually came into the room to say goodnight or to quiet them if they were making too much noise. He would find them both doubled over laughing, holding their stomachs and howling for mercy. Alfie was pleased that his father was easy-going. If his mother had been alive it would probably have been different. He missed her, even though he could hardly remember her. She had died when he was only two. Now he lived with his father in a village a couple of miles outside Wyckerton.

Alfie stared out of his window watching the birds while Derek lay reading on the spare bed.

Alfie knew that Derek and his family lived in the city, where his parents, Mr and Mrs Bodley, ran a Bed and Breakfast – B&B – called The Haven. Because Derek had two annoying younger sisters, Pippa and Fizz, he argued that staying at Alfie's house was the best option.

Alfie disagreed. Now that he was eleven, the thought of being in a city during the evening was much more exciting than being in a village where nothing happened. Pippa and Fizz weren't a problem whenever he saw them in Wyckerton during the day. Every time he walked past Derek's B&B he knew that, even if Pippa and Fizz were annoying, he would gladly put up with them in order to stay overnight in Wyckerton. He was annoyed that Derek refused to discuss it. Alfie had tried every angle he could think of. Being Alfie, that was a lot of angles. It was as if Derek had an off-switch like a toy when Alfie asked about staying at his B&B.

Pippa and Fizz weren't Derek's only excuse. He would say that Mrs Bodley was very busy. Or that the B&B was full of guests throughout the summer or that the B&B was being re-decorated. The list went on and on. Derek's excuses had been going on for so long that Alfie almost gave up.

Watching Wyckerton made Alfie ask again even though he already knew the answer.

'Derek, I don't understand *why* you always stay at my house. It would be awesome to stay in the city at your parent's B&B.' He visualized the huge, intriguing black and white building. A bubble of hope grew in Alfie's stomach but as Derek breathed in, the hope disappeared. He waited for one of the inevitable excuses.

'You know my Mum's busy with my sisters and the B&B,' muttered Derek.

'I just want to stay overnight in the B&B,' said Alfie, leaving out that it would be the stepping-stone to staying in Wyckerton. 'You've never even invited me in during the day. It's not fair. You stay at my house all the time.'

Alfie waited for a reply. Nothing. Derek's off-switch had been activated. Derek jumped up and stomped into the bathroom to get ready for bed.

Alfie clenched his teeth together. *Best friends should talk about everything.* He walked towards the door. *If you can't be bothered to talk to me, you can stay in here on your own,* he thought, planning to go and find something to eat. His leg knocked Derek's overnight bag, which was balanced on a chair. A book fell out. He picked it up, intending to put it back. *Odd title,* he thought, *"How Dragons Hide from Non-Magics."* He couldn't help opening it. He started to read:

> *Dragons were hunted to near-extinction by non-magics. Through the centuries their numbers have become dangerously low. The dragons had to take action before it was too late. The dragons have, so far, managed to survive by learning to disguise themselves. Even while flying on their brooms, wizards rarely report seeing them. The dragons…*

Derek made Alfie jump when he slammed the book shut and snatched it out of Alfie's hands.

'What are you doing? That's my book,' Derek's voice was tense.

'Sorry, it fell out of your bag. What's it about?'

Derek looked worried. 'Um… How much did you read?'

'Only a little bit. What are non-magics?' asked Alfie.

Derek's body stiffened. 'They're…' His voice trailed off.

Alfie felt his eyes widen as he remembered what else he'd read. 'Are there really *wizards*?' The idea was awesome.

'Don't be daft. It's a children's book.'

'It didn't seem like it,' he said. 'There were no pictures. The writing was grown-up.'

Derek bit his bottom lip, which was something he did if he was worried. Alfie spotted it and dared to hope that wizards might exist.

'It… it's just made up … that dragons … it's just pretend!' stuttered Derek.

'Let me see it again.' Alfie held out his hand.

'No! It's not mine, I have to give it back.' Derek shoved it to the bottom of his bag. He stubbornly zipped it up, then grabbed the handles and put the bag on the end of his bed before he slid under the covers.

'Night.' He turned away from Alfie, making it clear that he didn't want to talk.

The muscles tightened in Alfie's throat. He was too angry to speak. The gentle rhythmic sound of Derek's breathing floated around the room but it was far too quick for Derek to have fallen asleep. He watched the duvet rise and fall and shook his head in disbelief.

He went down to the kitchen, his feet slapping noisily on the tiled floor. He grabbed a packet of biscuits, shoved one after another into his mouth and swallowed the milky mixture as his mind drifted. What he had read was puzzling, but Derek's excuse was weirder. It didn't explain anything. His fingers dipped back into the packet, struggling to get another biscuit but the packet was empty. If he couldn't read the book again, he'd have to let it go. He felt his arms twitch. He wasn't good at letting things go.

His mind buzzed as he went upstairs to the bathroom and changed into his pyjamas. If he pretended witches and wizards really did exist, things started to make sense. Wizards flew around on brooms. Maybe the strange birds he had watched flying over Wyckerton were wizards. His stomach fizzed with excitement. He had to read Derek's book properly. It might even mention Wyckerton.

Alfie tiptoed over to Derek's bed and slipped his hand into Derek's bag. He dug deep, passed the soft clothes, smiling to himself as he felt the hard corner of the book. His fingers wouldn't fit underneath.

Derek stirred and slowly rolled over. Alfie held his breath and gently eased his arm out of the bag. He moved closer to Derek's face and waved his hand in front of his eyes. Derek didn't move. Alfie slipped his hand back into the bag. The book was shoved so far under everything he couldn't get a proper grip. He wriggled and pushed, trying to get hold of the book, as he struggled the bag pushed against Derek's foot.

Derek woke immediately. 'What are you doing?' he exploded.

Alfie's arm was stuck. He tugged it out of the bag, knowing he'd been caught red-handed. He didn't bother denying it.

'I need to see your book. It will help me understand…'

Derek grabbed his bag and found the book. He shoved it under his pillow, then thumped his head down on top.

'I told you. It's not my book. It's a story, Alfie. Go to bed.'

Alfie wondered why Derek was so grumpy. What was he hiding?

'I just want to find out more about wizards.'

'Don't make this into your next case. It's just a book. Leave it!' Derek sounded angry.

It wasn't worth arguing when Derek was like this. Alfie admitted that he could be a bit annoying. He couldn't stop snooping but Derek usually loved helping him solve mysteries.

Alfie remembered how much his chest had hurt the day they had run away from the paperboy who hadn't been doing his job properly. The villagers had been moaning about the unreliable deliveries. He figured out that it was the paperboy. He and Derek needed proof. They had followed him the next morning and had caught him dumping the newspapers on an old man's compost heap. The old man hadn't noticed the extra papers as he composted them anyway. The paperboy could have been a bull as he'd chased them through the village. Alfie's lungs had felt as though they were going to burst. He had felt safer with Derek by his side but they'd still run away, laughing with relief when they'd escaped. They always watched out for each other.

Alfie's father had revealed another mystery when he had mumbled that their milk often tasted sour or weak. Alfie unsuccessfully pondered the problem until Derek had said that it was going to snow. *That meant footprints – perfect.* After the milkman had delivered the milk, they'd snuck outside before anyone else was around. They'd followed an extra set of footprints in the snow and caught a man taking new milk bottles and replacing them with his old, watered-down ones. A thief. He was cheating his neighbours.

Alfie's favourite mystery had been at school. Lunch money had gone missing from pupils' drawers. Alfie had come up with a plan. They'd dipped some coins in weak ink so that the thief would have stained hands. They'd been thrilled when it turned out to be Edward and John, the school bullies. They had received a weeks' detention. Luckily, they never found out that it was Alfie and Derek who had trapped them.

Alfie sighed. He relied on Derek. Derek was the steady one. He looked at problems from a different angle, plodding along, gathering information. Sometimes adding the last few bits of information so that they could see the whole picture. They made a really good team.

Derek had acted so strangely about the dragon book, Alfie was sure that there was another mystery. He sighed, sad that he had to solve this one alone. Now he needed to prove it. If he could stay in Wyckerton just once, maybe he'd discover the answer.

Alfie tiptoed to his bed. The covers felt cool as they slid up his legs. The weird birds came back into his mind. They were odd, not really like birds at all. *Why don't I ever see them during the day? In daylight they wouldn't be such dark, mysterious shapes.*

He rubbed his temples as he remembered Derek's book. Most of the books he'd seen about dragons were for children, full of colourful pictures and stories of how they lived. The little bit of Derek's book that he'd read described how dragons were hunted by non-magics and how they now disguised themselves to survive. The book told the reader that dragons were in danger because of non-magics. Derek had lied. It wasn't a storybook. Alfie was certain of that.

The book also mentioned wizards flying on broomsticks. He started to get muddled as he imagined strange birds that became witches and wizards flying over Wyckerton. Though he tried to keep his eyelids open, they closed as he drifted off to sleep.

*

Alfie's bedroom was dark apart from the moonbeams that shone through the crack left by the curtains. Their light spread softly around the room and made everything faintly visible but drained of colour.

Alfie slept soundly that fateful Friday night. In the early hours of the morning he fidgeted. His face twitched, smiled and, at least twice, beamed. He usually woke up with a groan, stirring as the roughly closed curtains let the morning light flicker across his eyelids. Today he woke early. His eyes snapped open. He knew a secret. Every molecule of his body bubbled but his mind refused to remember.

As the fug in his brain cleared, he sat bolt upright. *Blimey!* he thought, looking towards Derek's bed. He was fast asleep with his mouth wide open. Alfie flung his covers back and crossed the room in two strides. His pointed finger pushed through muscle before it jabbed the bone of Derek's arm.

Derek's whole body jumped away subconsciously.

'OW!' he shouted as he woke up and scowled at Alfie.

'*Now* I know why I never get to stay at your B&B!' Alfie didn't have time for niceties.

'What?' demanded Derek.

'Wyckerton! There are witches and wizards living there among the ordinary people. During the day they act as if they're normal but at night, when the non-magic people have left, they live as wizards!' Alfie felt his throat shrink with excitement.

Derek looked him straight in the eye. His lower jaw moved forward.

'*What* are you talking about?' he growled. 'Don't be stupid!' His untidy dark hair sat like a cloud over his astonished face.

Alfie's cheeks ached. His smile couldn't stretch any wider. 'I *know* …' he repeated quietly. 'I dreamt about it.'

'Oh, that makes it true then,' Derek's voice dripped with sarcasm.

'It explains why you always stay at my house,' Alfie's voice rose. 'You live in a huge Bed and Breakfast yet there's never enough room for me! I don't know why I've never thought of it before.'

Derek was defensive. 'What, that I live in a city full of wizards? Heck, Alfie, do you believe in fairies, too?'

'Not fairies but what I dreamt was real!'

'How can *that* be real? What other crazy things were in it?'

'That I'm a wizard too. I can do magic…' as the words left his mouth, a warm feeling pulsed through Alfie's veins.

Derek shook his head.

'Do you know how daft you sound?' The look on Derek's face warned him not to argue.

Alfie felt his jaw stiffen. *Okay*, he thought. *You always want proof so I'll get you proof!* He knew there was no way he was going to win this dispute without it.

CHAPTER TWO

Let The Magic Begin

ALFIE spent the morning wondering how he was going to prove that Wyckerton was a magic city. It seemed impossible. Every thought had a dead-end. The smell of bacon and eggs from the kitchen brought them downstairs before they were called.

Alfie was still puzzled as he walked into the kitchen. 'Morning, Dad,' he mumbled.

His father was idly turning the bacon in the frying pan. 'Morning.' He served up the meal and brought it to the table. He plonked two plates down and went back for his own. When he sat down, they started to eat.

'Are you alright, Dad?' asked Alfie, uneasy with his father's silence. He was usually full of energy but his shoulders were slightly hunched. His face was dark with stubble.

Alfie felt a pang of guilt for wanting to stay elsewhere. His father was the best in the world. He was always there for him, willing to help with his homework or play ball when he needed a partner. He tried his hardest to make home a happy place. He was a great cook and he always did the ironing on Sunday evening. It wasn't that Alfie didn't enjoy being there, it would be better with more people around.

His father had told him that his mother had been thrilled when he was born. They had both wanted the house to be full of children. Alfie looked at his father. He deserved to be happy. Alfie closed his eyes. He didn't want to think about it. They had both lost so much when his mother had died.

His father took a deep breath as he ran a huge hand through his short, blonde hair. Alfie watched each chopped strand flick upright as it escaped. He'd never noticed that they had the same hair until now. Alfie's was longer but still as coarse and thick. He looked at his father properly. He was really strong. Alfie couldn't imagine ever having muscles that big. He was skinny. Even his bones had bones. He looked at Derek. His bones were covered with muscle and didn't look as knobbly as Alfie's.

Alfie's father cleared his throat, 'Alfie, I've been asked by my company to head a new venture in China. It's a two-year contract. I'll constantly be moving around the country.' His voice sounded weary.

Alfie was shocked. He didn't want to move away.

'What about me?' he asked. He didn't want to go to China. He wanted to live in Wyckerton. Why had this happened? He had to stay and enjoy the magical city now that he knew about it.

Before his father could answer Derek spoke, 'It will be horrible if you leave.'

'I don't want to,' said Alfie.

Alfie's father rubbed his chin. 'I'm worried about you and your future. It won't be good for you to leave England and travel with me. You're about to start senior school. Getting a good education is really important. So I've decided to go into Wyckerton to ask Derek's parents if you can stay with them.'

Alfie's skin tingled with relief.

Derek looked horrified. 'No! I mean… I don't… I don't think he'll be able to. My parents are very busy at this time of year … my sister has been quite ill…' Words tumbled from Derek's mouth.

Alfie wasn't fooled any more. Derek's reply was predictable. He had to protect Wyckerton. If one of Derek's younger sisters had really been ill, Alfie would have known about it. The emotions shooting across Derek's face were very clear. He wanted to stop Alfie's father asking his parents.

Alfie watched his father's chin wrinkle. 'I still need to go and ask them,' he said.

Derek shook his head.

Go Dad! thought Alfie. He was glad that grown-ups didn't always listen to children.

The afternoon dragged. When Alfie's father called upstairs that he was ready to leave for Wyckerton, Alfie carefully put his wallet in his pocket. He walked into the hall as Derek was tying his laces.

'Your Dad's left. He said to catch him up.'

Alfie slipped on his shoes. Excited now that he had a plan, he felt a shiver run down his spine. *If I'm going into Wyckerton, I'm not coming out again until I see the truth.* He intended to hide his wallet near the B&B. When he left the city with his father, he would pretend he'd lost it, have to go back, and end up staying in Wyckerton till late.

He bent to tie his laces but stopped mid-way. They were already tied. 'Did I do them up?' he said aloud, wondering if he had forgotten.

Derek was pale. 'H…how did you do them up?' he stuttered.

'What?'

'How did you do them up – you didn't even touch them?'

'Don't be daft. Of course I tied them, I just forgot.' Alfie stood up, shrugged and headed outside. He glanced back. Derek was standing still.

'What's wrong?' asked Alfie.

'What?' Derek looked confused. 'Oh … nothing.' He still didn't move.

'Come on then, slow coach!' called Alfie as he walked off, eager to get to the city.

Alfie's father was ahead of them. Alfie loved the trees that overhung the road that led into Wyckerton, especially at this time of year. The sun shimmered through the thick, green leaves making them glow. Derek dawdled, set on holding them back.

Suits me, thought Alfie, *the later we're in Wyckerton the better.* Alfie lost sight of his father as they walked through the arched gateway into the city. *I'm in Wyckerton now and I'm not leaving until I've seen the truth.* Alfie's mood kept switching between happy and worried. He wondered if Derek's parents would allow him to stay. If they wouldn't let him stay, then he really needed his plan to work to prove that Wyckerton was a magic city.

He stopped to watch a cat with four kittens, all tottering behind her. Derek stopped beside him. The kittens struggled over the bottom bar of a gate and one by one wiggled through a cat-flap. The cat jumped through before the last kitten. She pulled her leg free as the flap snapped shut. The flap was stuck. The last kitten couldn't push through. It started to meow loudly. Alfie could see the mother trying to push the flap from the inside.

'I think the cat-flap's broken,' said Alfie as he opened the gate.

'You can't just go into someone's garden,' said Derek as he followed nervously behind.

Alfie guided the kitten out of the way.

Derek tried the flap. It was wonky and stuck. The plastic hinges were damaged.

'It's definitely broken. I can't move it. The kitten will just have to wait for the owner to come back.'

'But something might hurt it without its Mum around.' Alfie bent down.

'Look. The hinges are holding it lopsided. If I twist it back, they'll break,' explained Derek.

'Let me try,' said Alfie.

Derek stood up grudgingly. 'You won't be able to fix it.'

Alfie struggled and almost gave up. Suddenly the flap moved and straightened, working perfectly. Pleased, he lifted the kitten and was amazed at how fragile it was. Its bones felt like egg shells. All its weight was in its fat little tummy. He plopped it through the flap.

'It was *really* broken. The hinges aren't even bent anymore…' Derek stared at him in disbelief. 'How did you do that?'

'Ha-ha. Magic!' said Alfie, stretching out his hands like a magician.

Derek looked uncomfortable but didn't answer. They walked along silently until they reached Derek's street. Alfie caught sight of his father. He stood by the B&B in the shadow of the heavy oak porch talking to Mrs Bodley. She had almost closed the door behind her and was casually leaning against the frame. Alfie felt that she was purposely blocking the entrance, just like Derek always did.

Alfie watched them, too nervous to breathe. His father's voice floated toward him.

'– and my company want me to start in a week. It's important that he starts senior school here.'

'Steven, you know we'd love to have him, it's just that…' Mrs Bodley faltered, then her nose wrinkled, 'business is really good at the moment. The B&B is always busy. We're full for the rest of the summer.'

'But they always share a room when Derek comes to us. Wouldn't that be possible?' Alfie's father looked hopeful.

Mrs Bodley faltered again as she spoke, 'Um … I'm not sure that would be good on a permanent basis, specially not on school nights.'

Alfie watched the frown on his father's face. As Alfie listened, he wondered why he had always believed Derek's excuses. Mrs Bodley was using exactly the same ones. Alfie tilted his head to the side. Her reasons were just reinforcing his dream. Why would Derek *and* his mother be worried about him staying, if it weren't true?

Alfie's father spoke again, 'I'm not sure who else to ask. I think staying in Wyckerton would be best for him.' He paused, giving Mrs Bodley the chance to change her mind but she didn't say anything. 'Okay,' he sighed. 'I'll have to reconsider taking him to China with me.' He tried to be positive.

Alfie felt his stomach lurch. 'I don't want to go!' he called out.

His father looked at him. 'We can discuss it at home, Alfie.' He glanced at his watch and turned to Mrs Bodley. 'It's getting late. I have a works event to attend this evening. Thank you, anyway. Bye.' He turned away and started to walk down the street. 'I won't be very late, Alfie. I'll see you at home, unless Mrs Bodley lets you stay here tonight,' he called as he disappeared around the corner.

Mrs Bodley was still blocking the doorway to the B&B. Alfie knew she wasn't going to invite him to stay.

She looked at Derek. 'Derek, do you want to have another sleepover at Alfie's tonight?'

'Yeah, okay,' said Derek.

Mrs Bodley smiled at Alfie before she backed into the B&B and firmly closed the front door. *That makes the fourth night in a row that he's stayed with us. Let me stay here.*

Alfie glanced at Derek. He was trying to loosen cobbles with his shoe but it was too big to get underneath them. Alfie tucked his wallet behind the bush by the front door, pleased that his plan could still work. If he managed to stay in Wyckerton until late, he would see everyone become witches and wizards. Excitement bubbled as he tried to imagine it.

'Let's go back to your house. We could have a game of football,' Derek sounded eager.

Ah, time to leave Wyckerton. Alfie walked slowly trying to stretch out the journey.

'I'd like to start senior school here.' Alfie felt gloomy, the threat of moving away suddenly seemed real.

'It will be really different without you.' Derek looked sad. 'You've been my best friend since we were five.'

Six years, thought Alfie, *and I've never seen inside the B&B.* 'I suppose you'll make a new best friend.'

'Not one as good as you.' Derek reassured him. 'I guess Bun and Chris will be at senior school, though.'

'Who are they?' asked Alfie, puzzled that Derek hadn't mentioned them before.

'Two boys from the city. They're good fun. Chris is huge, like a rugby player. Everyone moves out of his way as he walks along.' Derek smiled before he added, 'But he wouldn't hurt a fly.'

Alfie imagined a crowd of people separating to let Chris through. 'What about Bun?' he asked.

'Bun is … well … he's the Persuader.'

Alfie was baffled. 'What?'

'He's amazing. He comes up with solutions so quickly. He's saved us from loads of sticky situations. Somehow, he can make adults do what he wants them to do. They think he's adorable.' Derek pulled a face and shook his head in disbelief. 'It even works on my Mum. Once, when she was too busy to bake, he said that her cakes were the best he'd ever tasted. Guess what? Right there and then she made a huge chocolate cake for him. I've tried that loads of times but she ignores me!'

Alfie laughed.

'Mum says he's charming!' said Derek. 'They went to a different primary school, but they'll go to my senior school.' He seemed pleased at the thought.

Alfie had never really thought about other primary schools. 'Why did you come out to my village's school and not go to one in Wyckerton?'

'Mum wanted me to mix with non – ' Derek slammed his mouth shut. His eyes opened so wide they nearly fell out of their sockets.

Alfie laughed at Derek's look of horror. 'Non – what?' he asked, and hoped it was *Non-magics*. He'd read that word in Derek's book.

'I meant people not from the city.'

'Why would that start with non?' asked Alfie.

Derek fidgeted and bit his bottom lip.

Alfie's eyes half-closed as he recognised Derek's habit. He always bit his lip when he was nervous. Alfie kept quiet.

Derek had to answer. 'Non-city dwellers,' said Derek and puffed out the rest of his breath.

Alfie's lips twitched. He didn't know whether to laugh or be annoyed that Derek was lying to him. He turned away and started to walk quickly. Then he slowed down when he remembered that he needed to waste time.

'The kittens must still be inside,' said Alfie as they passed the house with the cat flap. He caught Derek looking at him oddly. He stopped walking.

'That cat-flap was definitely broken. How did you mend it?' asked Derek. He seemed deadly serious, as if he was struggling to understand something.

'I think it was just stuck. You were probably pushing it the wrong way.' Alfie wondered what Derek meant.

'And your shoe laces? They did themselves up.' Derek's head moved forward as he spoke.

'What! No they didn't, I must have done them – you just didn't see.'

Derek shook his head.

Alfie didn't have time to think about it. It was far more important that his plan worked ... that he stayed in Wyckerton until late.

They started walking again and were very close to the city entrance. Alfie stopped to look at his watch. *Almost six o'clock.*

Derek grabbed Alfie's sleeve and tugged.

'I'm getting hungry. Hurry up.'

Alfie twisted his upper body sharply and Derek lost his grip. Alfie started to pat his pockets. He opened his eyes wide.

'Oh no! I've lost my wallet. I think it fell out near your B&B,' he shouted. He turned and started to run through the streets towards the B&B. He saw Derek's confused look before he followed.

At the B&B Alfie found his wallet under the bush and slipped it in his pocket. He pretended to be looking for it as Derek arrived.

'Why do you think it's here?'

'I think I felt it fall out when my father was talking to your mother.'

'Why didn't you look at the time?' snapped Derek.

'I forgot.' Alfie felt awful lying to Derek. He looked up and caught Mrs Bodley gaping through the window like a fish in a bowl.

She made her way towards the front door and spoke before it was fully open. 'Derek,' her voice was harsh, 'why are you still here? I thought you were going to stay at Alfie's.'

'Alfie lost his wallet.' Derek spoke quickly.

'You should have left the city by now.'

Alfie saw a man and woman walking together on the other side of the street, and two businessmen walking towards him. They were all wearing jackets made of similar cloth.

'We were almost out of the city when Alfie ran back here,' explained Derek to Mrs Bodley as if he expected to be told off.

Mrs Bodley looked confused. She started to shake her head. 'Has he ever been in Wyckerton this late?' she asked.

'No,' said Derek.

As Derek spoke, Alfie heard a bell toll. He followed Derek's gaze towards the couple, who were a little further down the road. The bell chimed again. As it rang out for the third time, the couple's jackets changed into cloaks. The fabric was the same but the colours were more intense.

Alfie's jaw dropped as he stared at them. They were wizards. He spun around to look at the two businessmen. They were also wearing cloaks. The deep reds, golds and greens of the cloaks reminded Alfie of autumn leaves.

Mrs Bodley anxiously shouted into the hallway of the B&B, 'Peter! Come here, quickly!'

Mr Bodley came to the door. He smiled at his wife who jutted her head towards Alfie.

'What?' Mr Bodley was shocked. 'No ... he can't still be here.'

'Well, he is,' stated Mrs Bodley. 'And the bell has tolled.' She seemed puzzled.

'But ... Oh, I don't understand.' Mr Bodley looked dazed. He sat down on a bench by the front door. He looked totally flummoxed as he tried to grasp what had happened.

'I knew it, I *knew* it!' shouted Alfie, feeling as though his blood would boil ... that he would explode.

His dream was true. Wyckerton was a magic city.

Derek spoke slowly, almost to himself, 'Unbelievable ... how ...' he shook his head as if he was trying to figure something out. 'Well ... it's the only solution,' he whispered.

'What's the only solution?' asked Alfie.

Derek looked up. 'You said you knew about Wyckerton this morning. I didn't believe you. Sorry.'

'Knew what about Wyckerton?' interrupted Mrs Bodley.

'That the witches and wizards don't have to pretend to be normal when all the non-magics have left the city for home,' said Derek.

'Non-magics don't know that. They never even think about it.' Mrs Bodley sounded certain.

'I know. That's what I didn't understand, until strange things started happening today.'

'What sort of things?' asked Mrs Bodley, trying to make sense of it.

'When we were getting ready to leave Alfie's house, he put on his shoes and the laces tied themselves,' said Derek.

Alfie laughed.

'They didn't tie themselves,' mocked Alfie. 'I did them without thinking!' He didn't know why Derek was so focussed on his laces.

Mrs Bodley ignored Alfie and nodded to encourage Derek to continue. 'And he mended a cat flap that was definitely broken.'

Alfie shook his head. 'It obviously wasn't ... how could I have just *fixed it*?' he scoffed.

'Well... if you add all the things together, shoelaces and the cat flap, plus that the Charm on the city hasn't made you leave, there's only one solution,' repeated Derek.

Mrs Bodley's hand flew up to cover her mouth as she gasped.

Mr Bodley jumped up from the bench and stood there, open-mouthed.

'What?' Alfie spoke slowly.

'Alfie, you're a wizard,' stated Derek. 'You *are* magic!'

CHAPTER THREE

Park Your Broomstick

EVEN though Alfie had just witnessed men changing into wizards and women changing into witches, Derek's statement was incredible.

'WHAT?' said Alfie. 'That can't be true!'

'You were doing those things magically,' insisted Derek.

'No…' Alfie felt confused. *Of course I'm not magic … that's ridiculous!* He was shocked by what was happening around him. 'I knew witches and wizards lived in Wyckerton, but me … that's impossible.' Even though he had been a wizard in his dream, he couldn't believe it.

'How would you explain those things, then?' asked Derek.

'Well … eh … they were just weird … I can't …' Alfie stuttered.

'It was actually because you're magic. The Charm never lies.' Derek was certain, he seemed to have it all sorted out.

'That's true,' said Mrs Bodley. 'The Charm protects the city. When the bell rings the all clear we know that *all* the non-magics have left the city. If you were a non-magic, Alfie, you wouldn't still be here.'

Mr Bodley nodded. 'There's no other explanation.'

But …but, thought Alfie.

Mrs Bodley walked towards him. He half-stepped back as she reached out. His lower lip pulled down as his hands moved up to protect himself. Her arms surrounded him in a hug. It almost hurt. His body was squashed as if he were a mouse squeezing through a drinking-straw. Deep in his mind a memory sparked with recognition. This was a motherly hug. He relaxed into it and didn't want her to let go.

Mrs Bodley spoke softly, 'We were always concerned with getting you out of the city and home safely. I never considered that you belong here.'

She stepped back towards the front door.

'It makes a huge difference.' She looked relieved. 'We don't have to worry about you staying here now. Come in.' She turned around, went into the hall and walked towards the back of the house. The front door was open, leaving the entrance clear.

Alfie felt lightheaded. He struggled to take in everything that had been said. For the first time ever he had been invited into the B&B. He was stunned. He couldn't move. The black and white building looked ancient. The timber frame that held the walls together was black from age, the grain dried out and rough. The white plaster between the timbers was painted and gleamed in the sunlight. He had to squint to protect his eyes from its brightness.

'Are you alright?' Mr Bodley seemed concerned.

'I'm a bit shocked,' responded Alfie.

'Me too. We didn't have a clue.' Mr Bodley started to laugh. He looked happy again.

Alfie laughed too.

'Hello, Nigel.' Derek's voice was warm as he greeted an approaching man.

Alfie stared at the distinguished-looking man. He was a real wizard. Nigel wore a black tapestry cloak that shimmered with gold and underneath long flowing robes of burgundy. His curly, greying hair suited his kind face. Alfie felt the aura of calm about him.

Nigel chuckled. 'Hello, Derek.'

'This is Alfie.' Derek introduced him. 'He's going to stay with us.'

'Oh…' Nigel looked at him. 'Pleased to meet you, son.' He offered his hand for Alfie to shake, each ridge of his knuckles looked huge. Alfie shook the cool, long fingers. Nigel's warm, brown eyes were friendly as he smiled. Alfie managed a weak smile before he turned back and looked at the open door of the B&B.

Derek said quietly, 'The buildings have more fitting names at night, too.'

Alfie looked above the door at the sign saying, *Park Your Broomstick*. He shook his head in disbelief. Whenever he'd read it before it had said, *The Haven*.

The open front door left a large hole. The doorframe was thick wood. It ran up both sides and met in a point at the top, like an upside down V. Alfie walked to the door and looked in, unsure of what to expect.

Derek joined him. They went into the entrance hall. Alfie immediately felt the calmness, as if the house was content. The walls on either side of him were made of small, dark panels of wood. *If Henry VIII walked in now, it wouldn't seem odd,* he thought, looking around. He took another step. A central staircase and four doors led from the entrance hall to other rooms, one door in each corner. A heavy honey aroma hung in the air from the beeswax furniture polish.

The wooden panelling made it darker. He squinted toward the door on his right. As he moved closer he realised that it wasn't a door at all, it was a bookcase. *How could I have been so stupid?* He wondered if Derek had noticed his mistake. His cheeks burned as they turned red. He pretended that he wanted to look at the books. They were all very old and made of leather. He reached up to touch one.

'Good, aren't they?' Derek arrived at his side and found a handle. He pushed the door open. 'Obviously, this is the study.'

Not obvious at all. Alfie still felt rather stupid.

'The doors hint at the room they lead into,' explained Derek. 'The wood is carved with the shapes of the things that are in that room. I like the kitchen door best. It's covered in wooden cakes,' said Derek, with a smile. He showed Alfie around the study.

'Derek, can you show Alfie to his room. He can have one of the smaller ones or you can share the big room at the back on the third floor,' said Mrs Bodley, poking her head around the study door.

They looked at each other. Alfie knew what Derek was thinking – *no adults, talking loudly, playing late into the night, all topped with a midnight feast.* The opportunity was too good to miss.

'I'd prefer to share,' said Alfie.

Derek sniggered and gave him a sneaky thumbs-up.

'That's fine,' said Mrs Bodley as she disappeared.

'Come on, I'll take you up.' Derek ran toward the stairs.

Alfie dodged around pieces of furniture and followed him. They climbed up two old wooden staircases that took them to the second floor. On the long landing, Derek disappeared around a corner. Alfie followed slowly, treading down two shallow steps that took him around to the left. Then he went up three steep ones, which led to two corridors. He wondered which one to take when Derek poked his head out from behind a wall. Alfie hadn't noticed the other entrance. It was slightly along the right-hand corridor. He wondered how he'd ever find his way back downstairs.

'Up here,' said Derek.

Alfie ran to catch him. He peeped around the wall, thinking that Derek would jump out. Instead he found a narrower set of stairs. They were nothing like the elegant wooden ones he'd just run up. They were made of flagstones and should have been in a castle. He could only see four and a half steps because they circled around a brick centre post. As Alfie reached out his fingers splayed wide on the cold, smoothly painted bricks that curled around the stairs on both sides. The bottom rows of bricks were laid long and level, but as the wall rose higher, the bricks were laid at a slant. He climbed the hard, stone staircase. It was completely solid, unlike the wooden ones that moved slightly. At the top, the bricks were all standing bolt upright like soldiers. On the landing he called out to Derek, who'd disappeared again.

'In here!' shouted Derek and opened a heavy oak door leading to a large, comfortable room.

Alfie went in and sat on one of the beds, grateful for the rest. He hadn't known the B&B was so big.

He bounced. 'Mmm, comfy bed.'

'They adjust to the guest,' said Derek, 'just as soft as you want.'

Alfie shook his head in disbelief. He looked around the room. It was slightly worn in a welcoming kind of way. A deep red rug covered most of the dark, wide floorboards. His eyes wandered around the room and settled on the smooth plaster walls. They were painted a warm, light brown. He wanted to lick them to make sure they weren't covered in melted chocolate. *Now that would be magic.* He giggled to himself.

Fizz, Derek's five-year-old sister, appeared at the door.

'Pippa and I share too,' she said excitedly and bustled off again. Derek looked miffed.

'I forgot they were on this floor, I hope their room's a long way from ours. They'll probably be making a noise on the landing in the morning,' he moaned.

'I won't sleep in. Too much to explore,' said Alfie. He grinned as he jumped up to look around the room. A huge dresser took up most of the wall opposite the door. The twin beds and side tables were made of the same heavy wood. Two windows, made from small diamonds of glass, filled the wall between the beds. At the foot of each bed was a huge leather trunk.

Mr Bodley appeared at the door looking very relaxed in his cloak.

'I thought you might need some night clothes,' he said, and swished his hand gently. Alfie noticed a toothbrush and neatly folded pyjamas hovering behind him. They floated in through the door and settled on top of the dresser. 'We always keep a few bits handy for forgetful guests.' Mr Bodley smiled. 'Good choice of room,' he said as he left.

'I just watched your Dad perform magic!' shouted Alfie in disbelief.

'Yep,' said Derek, as if it were completely normal.

'I've known you for most of my life and you've never done anything magical.'

'It isn't allowed in front of non-magics. If we'd known about you, you could have stayed before.'

'I can't believe all this is happening,' said Alfie.

'Look, don't worry about it. You'll soon fit in.'

But how? He'd never consciously done anything magical in his life. Why should he be able to start now?

'Let's go downstairs. I'll show you around.' Derek seemed excited, as if he was pleased to be able to share his house with Alfie at long last.

The B&B was even better than Alfie had imagined.

They went all the way down to the ground floor. Derek showed him the rooms one by one. Alfie agreed with Derek about the decorated doors. The cakes that covered the kitchen door promised all sorts of temptations, making it his favourite. The last door at the back of the hall led to the sitting room. The door was open. Alfie felt the warmth of the sun as he entered. Through a huge floor-to-ceiling window he saw an old cedar tree. The branches held trays of greenery at their tips.

Inside the room, wide wooden planks covered the floor. There were no rugs. He wanted to curl up on one of the over-sized sofas. This room would always be welcoming.

Derek was trying to explain how many more rooms there were upstairs.

'Don't bombard the boy.' An old lady poked her head around the wing of a chair. 'It's too big to get used to in one go!'

Alfie hadn't realised anyone else was in the room.

'Hello,' she said, holding out her crooked, old hand in greeting. 'Everyone calls me Aunt Edith. Derek is my grandson.'

'Pleased to meet you,' said Alfie. 'May I call you Aunt Edith?'

'Of course.' She moved her head back to its previous comfortable position. The mass of white hair tied on top of her head puffed out like a pillow.

Alfie noticed a metal cage in a corner of the room. He wondered what it was doing in the sitting room.

'What lives in there,' he asked, 'and *where* is it?'

'It's Ernie's, our German Shepherd puppy,' said Derek. 'He's probably gone outside with Pippa and Fizz.'

Alfie shook his head. He didn't know that Derek had a puppy.

'Why does he need to be put in the cage?' asked Alfie.

'They feel safer. Besides they never mess in their own space,' explained Derek.

'Can we go and find him?' Alfie had always wanted a puppy.

'If you like.' Derek shrugged.

A noise in the distance grew louder. Alfie realised it was running feet and shouting, combined with laughter. A bundle of fur skidded around the corner and ran into the room, almost sliding to a halt before using the back of a sofa like a train buffer to eventually stop.

Ernie turned around as if daring Pippa and Fizz, who were following, to try and catch him. His tongue lolled out from the side of his mouth. He spread his huge front paws, put his head down between them and yapped. His tail wagged madly still stuck in the air.

'Ernie, no tearing around in here,' Derek tried to sound firm but he was grinning. 'He's supposed to behave inside the house,' he explained.

With a glint in his eye, Ernie yapped again.

'No!' said Derek and pointed his finger sternly. Ernie ignored him and strolled off towards his water bowl as if he were in charge, his floppy ears set at a jaunty angle.

Alfie happily played with Ernie until suppertime. He tried to teach him to shake paws. He wasn't interested. Everyone spoilt him, no matter what he did.

A gong rang out and echoed around the B&B. 'Supper's ready,' said Derek, and jumped up.

Alfie arrived late in the kitchen, as Ernie was too entertaining to leave. The seats at the long table were filled with wizards. He lingered by the door, unsure where he should sit. Then, like magic, the enchanted table extended to seat him. *Wow*, he thought, unable to speak as he sat down.

Mrs Bodley carried serving dishes to the table. Everyone helped themselves as they ate and chatted. Alfie had never sat at such a crowded table. So many people made the mealtime lively. At home, mealtimes were quiet. It was just him and his Dad and occasionally Derek. He looked around. The table was full of content witches and wizards all chatting to each other.

As the meal ended Alfie quietly said, 'Do you need help with the washing up?' He hoped his expression hid the fact that he hated the job.

'I have some help, thanks,' said Mrs Bodley, nodding towards the sink.

Alfie followed her gaze. Amongst the bubbles a brush merrily cleaned all the dishes, a tea towel then dried them before they stacked themselves neatly away.

Perfect! I'll never have to wash-up again.

Before bed, Alfie helped Derek put Ernie in his cage.

'Night, Ernie, sleep well,' whispered Alfie, but he was already fast asleep, his head resting on his massive paws.

As Alfie changed into his pyjamas he felt exhausted but was looking forward to tomorrow. Now he had proved that Wyckerton was a magic city he felt as if he had always been welcome. Derek answered Alfie's questions late into the night. Eventually, there was no answer. Sleepily, Alfie looked towards Derek's bed, content that he wasn't pretending to sleep. At last, Derek was more than happy to tell Alfie everything that he knew about Wyckerton.

CHAPTER FOUR

The Enchanted City

DURING breakfast the residents and guests sat down to eat together. They looked perfectly ordinary in their day clothes but Alfie knew they were witches and wizards, as non-magics couldn't stay overnight in Wyckerton. He enjoyed asking them about their own magic lives. The guests stayed at the B&B for different reasons.

A young man in a grey suit said, 'I have a business meeting in Wyckerton today. I only stayed last night but when I tell my wife about this old building, I know we'll be back soon.'

Alfie hardly recognised him as one of the wizards from the previous evening. He was ready to leave the B&B and looked uncomfortable dressed in ordinary clothes. His suit reminded Alfie that outside the front door, the city was already full of non-magics.

'We live in London,' said a middle-aged woman as she touched her husband's hand. 'We're here for a whole week.' She strung her words out and Alfie could feel her excitement. 'I've brought so many beautiful cloaks with me but I can't resist buying more,' she said and chuckled.

A small girl playing with her doll ran behind Alfie's chair. She had made a broomstick out of a pencil; shredded paper bristles were stuck to one end. The girl ran around the kitchen, pretending the doll and broom could fly.

Alfie watched as her father said, 'My wife and I both grew up in Wyckerton. We've lived amongst non-magics since we were married.' He looked at his young daughter. 'Our daughter went flying for the first time last night. We've brought her on a proper holiday so that she can see that magic is normal. She's started to perform it at home. Just little things so far,' he said proudly.

'How old is she?' asked Alfie.

'Almost three. We weren't sure when she'd start doing magic.'

'Why?' Alfie thought that when he had children he would encourage them to do magic the day they were born.

'She's our first child. We have non-magics living all around us. They're her friends. We use magic in our home. It's safe with special hexes protecting it.'

Alfie felt his brow furrow. 'What are hexes?'

'They can be longer lasting spells. If you want to protect a house, for example.'

Alfie nodded. 'Oh …'

'We couldn't take our daughter flying at home,' said the father.

'She was so excited she hardly slept a wink last night,' added his wife.

'You'll just have to come to Wyckerton more often,' suggested Alfie.

'I agree. We might even move back when she's older.'

Alfie realised how lucky he was to be staying in Wyckerton. He remembered the loud, melodious bell that he had heard the evening before. 'The city changed last night when that bell tolled. Is that the Charm? It makes a beautiful sound but how does it work?'

'It rings once at midday,' Mrs Bodley informed him, 'but around six o'clock every evening it rings three times to inform everyone in the city that all the non-magics have left. The city-dwellers can then freely start using magic away from the security of their houses.'

'Does no-one come into the city after the bell?' asked Alfie.

'Wyckerton is a very old, walled city. The ancient Charm prevents non-magic people entering after six o'clock.'

'That sounds impossible. What happens if they want to go to a restaurant or to a grocers?' Alfie couldn't believe that a charm could prevent that from happening. Then he remembered how his father always wanted to eat elsewhere. He never wanted to go into Wyckerton at night.

'The idea might occur to non-magics but it always seems a better option to go to the local grocers outside the city or visit that nice little restaurant in the next village,' said Mrs Bodley.

Derek explained, 'The Charm changes their mind before the thought ends.'

'That's wicked.' Alfie was impressed.

'No, that's *magic*,' corrected Derek.

Alfie smiled. *Of course it is.*

Mr Bodley said, 'Nigel told me yesterday about his friend, Richard...' The doorbell interrupted him.

Mrs Bodley stood up. 'I wonder if that's your father, Alfie,' she commented as she made her way towards the hall.

Alfie jumped up and followed her. He arrived at the entrance hall as she opened the door. His father stood on the doorstep. As Alfie moved closer he could hear him speaking.

'I'm sorry it's early but my company want us to leave today. Alfie needs to come home now.'

Alfie ran the last few steps across the hallway.

'Dad, so much has happened since you left...'

'And what could that be?' asked his father, smiling.

Mrs Bodley spoke before Alfie had the chance to explain. 'We've discussed the possibility of Alfie staying here permanently. He and Derek have promised that it won't interfere with their schoolwork. If it's still an option, we would be pleased to have Alfie stay with us.'

Alfie was shocked and swung round to look at her.

'Really! I can live in Wyckerton?'

'If you abide by the rules,' said Mrs Bodley as she winked at him.

Alfie's hand shot up to his mouth. He had been about to blurt out Wyckerton's secret to his father.

'That would be most appreciated. Thank you.' Alfie's father's shoulders sank with relief. He looked at Alfie. 'If that's what you really want? You could come to China with me.'

'Wyckerton, please!' Alfie grinned but it faded slowly as he remembered that his father would be leaving soon. 'Will you be alright?' he asked.

Alfie's father put his hand on Alfie's head and ruffled his coarse blond hair.

'If I know you're safe and happy, I'll be fine. I promise I'll come back as often as I can.'

'And I'll work my hardest at school!' said Alfie.

'What! No daydreaming?' Alfie's father laughed.

'I'll try.' Alfie giggled. He couldn't promise. He also had magic to learn now.

'I'll go home, get your belongings and bring them back later,' said Alfie's father.

Mrs Bodley interrupted, 'Don't you worry about that! Peter can go over and collect them. You have enough to do. You'll need all the time to get ready for your flight.' She started to move back into the hall.

Alfie's father held out a house key and a wodge of money. 'Let me leave this for Alfie's expenses. I'll send more later.' He looked sad as he slowly said, 'I won't be there when you buy your school uniform. I'd been looking forward to doing that with you.'

Alfie heard the crack in his father's voice. They always bought things for the new school year together. He realised what a huge change to their lives this would be. He looked up at his father and moved closer for a hug. Slowly, they moved apart and Alfie's father ruffled his hair again. It was hard for him to turn and leave after they'd said goodbye.

For the second time in two days Alfie looked at the empty road where his father had been. His throat felt tight as his sight blurred. He felt alone and wondered if he'd made the right decision.

Mrs Bodley touched his shoulder.

'Come on, let's finish breakfast,' she said gently, and started to walk across the hall.

Alfie stood a little bit longer. He strained to hear his father's footsteps but they were too far away. He stepped back into the hall, closed the door and returned to the kitchen.

Later, as they prepared to go to his house, Alfie followed Derek and Mr Bodley into the entrance hall. He recognised the shuffling sound as post was shoved through the front door. He jumped as the letterbox turned into a mouth and started to gnarl at the paper, tearing some of it to shreds before swallowing it.

'What's happening?' he shouted as one letter was flung out onto the mat, untouched.

'That's the letter filter,' said Derek.

'What's it for?' asked Alfie, staying well away from the front door.

'It sorts the proper letters from the useless ones. Any that we don't want, it chews up and eats.'

Alfie chuckled. Now that would be the perfect present for his father. He was always moaning about the amount of rubbish that came through the letterbox.

Derek picked up the letter and placed it on a tray on the sideboard. He opened the front door and they made their way towards Alfie's village.

They spent the rest of the day at Alfie's house. He could see that his father had packed in a hurry before rushing to the airport. Alfie went into his father's room and closed the wardrobe door so that it looked as if he were still there.

Collecting his things together, he was amazed how much stuff he owned. He hunted around for some bags to hold his clothes, shoes and other possessions.

'Here, use this.' Mr Bodley handed him a folded rucksack as he and Derek started to pack some clothes.

'How are we going to carry all of this?' asked Alfie, looking at the bulging rucksacks.

'Well, you can probably manage two. Derek and I will take one each,' said Mr Bodley.

Alfie frowned. That was hardly fair, even though it was all his stuff. He saw Derek exchange a look with Mr Bodley. *Okay, I'll have a go.* He bent his knees, put his arms around an upright rucksack and heaved as he stood up. It shot into the air as if it weighed nothing. Alfie fell over.

Derek and Mr Bodley exploded with laughter.

Alfie stood up and lifted the rucksack with one hand. 'Wow! It's as light as my pillow.'

'They're LITE bags. You can fill them up and they never get heavy,' said Derek.

Alfie looked at the name written in huge letters, running down the side.

'Wizards use them if they go on walking holidays because they look normal,' said Mr Bodley. 'You both carry one. I'll take the other two. We don't want to draw attention to ourselves.'

Mr Bodley made sure the house was secure before he locked the front door.

'I expect your father will consider renting out the house now,' said Mr Bodley.

'Probably,' said Alfie. He looked at the house. In one day his life had completely changed.

A few villagers were outside as they walked down the front path. Mr Bodley struggled with the two bags. He could hardly get through the garden gate.

'Aren't they LITE bags?' whispered Alfie, confused as he read the name on them.

'Yes,' said Mr Bodley. 'But we don't want non-magics to know that, do we?'

'Oh yes.' Alfie immediately pretended his rucksack was really heavy.

They made it back to the B&B only minutes before suppertime. Collecting his possessions had taken longer than he'd hoped and he still had to unpack. Alfie wanted to explore the city after all the non-magics had left. So far he had only had a small glimpse on his first night. He sighed. He'd have to wait but knowing Derek, when he eventually showed him, it would be the best planned tour possible.

When Mrs Bodley rang the meal gong, Alfie and Derek sat at the table. Fewer guests were eating with them so the enchanted table remained its normal length. Alfie was starving and was pleased to see the huge amount of food. Dishes were filled with roast potatoes and vegetables. Three plates of steaming, roasted meats were waiting for Mr Bodley to carve. Alfie wondered if he could try them all. He opted to start with beef, his favourite. He filled his plate hoping there wouldn't be room for vegetables but Mrs Bodley insisted he took one of each colour. Alfie squeezed carrots, broccoli and parsnips onto his plate, huffing as they spread out over the beef and potatoes. Luckily, the gravy was thick and disguised them.

Aunt Edith sat, gently pulling a well-worn bracelet on her wrist. It moved around and around, the glittering jewel appeared then slipped out of sight on the other side of her wrist.

She coughed gently. 'I received a letter from my lawyers, Porter and Potts, this morning asking me to go to their offices and sign my will. They've finished making the changes,' she said.

'Oh, that's good,' said Mrs Bodley. 'When do you want to go? If you make it Tuesday, I can come with you.'

'I'd rather go tomorrow. I could go on my own.' Aunt Edith seemed defensive that Mrs Bodley thought she shouldn't go alone.

'It's quite a walk. Maybe Derek will go with you and keep you company.' Mrs Bodley gave Derek a look that warned him not to argue.

Derek slumped in his chair in protest. 'I'll go, if Alfie can come,' he said.

Aunt Edith seemed to perk up. 'It would be lovely to be accompanied by two young men,' she said. 'But I need to arrive after the bell has tolled.'

Alfie was excited. *At last, I'll finally see the city coming alive with witches and wizards.* He already knew some of the city during the day but tried to imagine how much it would change at night. By the time he went to bed, his brain was exhausted.

The next afternoon as they walked through Wyckerton with Aunt Edith, Alfie wasn't disappointed. His fingers itched to touch the buildings, in case they could pass on their knowledge. It occurred to him that they were privy to all sorts of magical scenes. Every night their surroundings changed from ordinary to magic. They would have witnessed centuries of witches flying past and wizards performing spells. The red bricks were speckled with orange and purple hues. They seemed to have their own aura as the sun hit the walls and made them glow, as if they were taking huge breaths in and out.

He followed Derek and Aunt Edith through the wide, cobbled streets. Even though some of them were familiar, it felt as though he was seeing them for the first time.

They hadn't gone too far from the B&B when Alfie stopped to look in a shop window. It was called Nurture by Nature and had a large display of open baskets full of grains, seeds and nuts. Beyond the glass window he could see bars of soap and tubs of lotion.

'All the shops look the same as they always did.' Alfie felt disappointed.

'Of course they do. The bell hasn't tolled,' said Aunt Edith. 'This is Nigel's shop. Such an honourable man. He's probably the city's best potion maker.' She seemed proud to be his friend.

Alfie looked at the two huge windows, one either side of the door. The glass gleamed in the sun. *Hmm, Potion-maker...?* It looked like a health food shop. 'Where are the potions, then?'

Aunt Edith tutted at having to explain again, 'Young man. They can't be on display now. They will be when all the non-magics have left and the shop becomes an apothecary called Powerful Potions.'

Alfie was taken aback. She seemed such a quiet old lady but she didn't disguise her irritation if she didn't like something.

'Can anybody own a shop?' he asked as they walked on.

'They're handed down through the family, just like Park Your Broomstick was,' answered Aunt Edith. 'But if there's no family, they do go up for sale.'

'Could it be bought by non-magics, then?' whispered Alfie.

'They come and look. Recently a shop came to the market. A particularly fat, wealthy non-magic wanted to buy it. He strutted around saying that he'd soon show us how to run a business properly. He bought everyone drinks at the tavern. When it was time to pay, he didn't have enough money. He left, feeling too embarrassed to return.' Aunt Edith chuckled at the memory.

'Did the city Charm make him lose his money?' asked Derek.

'Temporarily, yes,' she answered and stopped outside a house. Alfie couldn't understand why they'd stopped. It didn't look like a law firm's offices.

'This house is for sale,' she nodded towards a sign, 'and the estate agent must be inside as the door's open. Let's see what happens.' She seemed to be enjoying herself.

'Non-magics wouldn't be able to live in the city,' Derek reminded him.

'Whoever's in there with the estate agent can't be one of us. Obviously, any magics would look in the evening after the bell has tolled,' said Aunt Edith.

'How will non-magics be put off?'

'Let's go and find out.' Derek started to walk towards the open door. Alfie followed a few steps behind. They were about to stick their heads through the doorway to hear what was happening inside.

Alfie heard a female voice scream, 'Aah, A RAT! This house is disgusting. It said in the details that it was spotless!' She continued her outburst as she rushed out of the door, swerving to avoid Derek. 'There's far too much work to do before I could live there. And it's overpriced.'

'I'm sorry, madam, I thought that it was in a better condition,' said the agent. 'Of course, we'll inform you of any other houses for sale.'

'Don't bother. I've changed my mind about moving! I'm perfectly happy in the countryside,' she said as she stomped off down the road.

'Can't win them all, I suppose.' The agent looked at Alfie and Derek. 'Do you two live in the city?' he asked.

'Yes, at Park Your Broomstick,' answered Derek. 'Do you?'

'Yes,' said the agent, confirming that he was a wizard. 'More viewers are coming now. You'd better move along.' He raised his bushy eyebrows.

'Are they non-magics, too?' asked Alfie.

'Yes. It would put the city at risk if houses never came up for sale. We have to be willing to show non-magics around, even though there's no chance of them ever living here.'

'Can we watch how you do it?' Alfie was really interested.

'I suppose so. Not that I do anything,' said the agent. 'Here they are.' He walked towards the couple. 'Good afternoon, are you Mr and Mrs Brown?' He shook them by the hand. 'Now I think this house is just what you're looking for.' The agent took them towards the same house that he had showed his previous client.

'It looks perfect,' said the man. 'We're looking for somewhere in need of work. From the outside, this looks ideal.' They followed the agent through the front door.

'Oh no, they want a scruffy place with its own rats.' Alfie moved toward the door so he could hear what was being said.

Before he was able to get close, the couple came back outside. 'What a shame. It's immaculate. They've removed all the original features. Who would do that to such an old house?' said the man. 'It's not what we're after at all. It's ruined.'

Alfie moved out of the way.

'We won't bother looking at the rest of it,' said the man. They thanked the agent and went on their way.

'It can't be wrong for everyone, surely some non-magics will like it?' said Alfie, as the couple moved out of earshot.

'No, they see whatever they *don't* want to buy.' The agent jiggled his bushy eyebrows up and down. 'Now if you'll excuse me, I'll lock up and go back to my shop.'

They continued on their journey.

'Do you see how it works now, Alfie?' asked Aunt Edith.

'Yes. It's very complicated, though.'

'We don't have to worry about anything. The Charm does all the work.'

Alfie nodded. 'I suppose it does.' The non-magics hadn't questioned anything before they'd left.

As they passed the park, Alfie looked at the gigantic fountain. It was surrounded by clean, crystal-clear water that gleamed in the sun. Everything seemed different, brighter somehow. He'd been here plenty of times before with Derek but it was as if he'd worn blinkers.

'Come on Alfie, I want to show you the city change as the bell rings the all clear,' said Derek. 'It's so different when all the non-magics are gone.'

Aunt Edith strolled along behind them. They stopped by a pet shop and waited for the chimes to begin. Some kittens in the pet shop resembled little balls of coloured fluff, either curled up or wobbling around on short, skinny legs. Moving on to the next window Alfie noticed that it was full of household items.

The bell started to toll and Alfie grinned at Derek as the third chime sounded. The whole city seemed to take a deep breath and let go with relief as it shook off its daytime disguise.

Alfie squashed his nose on the shop window to get a better view. Rows of colourful cloaks and shelves full of pointed shoes, with buckles of all shapes and sizes, had replaced the household items. Masses of pointed hats were stacked against the back wall. He stepped back in a daze and looked at the sign above the shop door that said, *Nitty-Gritty – All Your Everyday Essentials.*

More like every night essentials, thought Alfie, smiling.

Wizards rushed out of buildings onto the streets. Some jumped on brooms and took flight. Children played with toys Alfie didn't recognise. A small group were playing cards. One player shouted 'Attack *you* with water!' and pointed a card at one of the other players. Water shot out of the card and drenched the boy as the others laughed.

Hope I can play that game one-day! Alfie laughed aloud.

He didn't know which way to look. He wished that he were an owl so that he could turn his head around and see everything at once.

A wizard ran along beside a broomstick as he taught his young son to fly. He wobbled and giggled as his mother stood on the pavement panicking.

'Be careful. Don't let him fall. Run faster!' She covered her eyes, too scared to watch.

A thin, bespectacled witch walked along. She carried a full shopping bag with one hand, and held her child's hand with the other. A book floated in front of her, the pages magically flipped over as she read.

Another witch stretched out of a window with a watering can. She watered the window box nearest her and then released the can so it floated towards some hanging baskets that she couldn't reach. She moved her empty hands as she magically guided it. It tipped the water into the baskets without spilling a drop.

Alfie started to walk along the street, trying to take it all in. The shops were far more exciting than usual now that they were selling magical products. Wizards bustled in and out of them, tempted by the items from shop windows or displays that spilled out onto the paths.

Exotic fruits were piled high outside a grocer shop. Large yellow, raspberry-shaped fruit took pride of place. 'Bananaberries. All the goodness of bananas and berries combined,' shouted the enthusiastic owner.

Strange plants, some of them moving, filled a table outside a flower shop. One seemed to be growing lumps of cheese. Underneath a sign said, *Get rid of those vermin with the new Venus Rat Trap.* Alfie shuddered, trying not to imagine what the plant did.

A sweet shop had a giant chocolate mallow outside. Adults and children surrounded it as they pulled off chunks to taste. Alfie watched as they struggled to break off more than one piece each. He realised it was impossible and smiled, admiring the shopkeeper's tactics as they entered the shop to buy more.

A toyshop advertised the latest version of *Classical Elements – the card game that will literally knock you off your feet!* Alfie was sure it was the same game he'd seen earlier.

He remembered the pet shop and rushed back. The multi-coloured kittens were replaced with jet black ones. They were still tottering around but somehow they didn't look so innocent.

The scene as he looked down the street was unbelievable. At night the city seemed older, as if it had stepped back in time. Tinted with a golden hue, the street was like an old photograph. He wanted to stand and watch forever. His skin tingled as he realised that this was only the beginning.

Derek and Aunt Edith had moved on. Grudgingly, Alfie followed and caught up with them.

'Impressed?' asked Derek, not doubting the answer.

'It's even better than I imagined,' said Alfie.

CHAPTER FIVE

Sibling Rivalry

AUNT Edith stopped beside a set of beautiful stone steps. They were wide and shallow as if most of the clients that used them were old. Iron railings ran along the front of the building and curved in to follow the steps up to the solid front door.

'Here we are.' Aunt Edith started up the steps. 'You can come in. It won't take long.' It seemed more like an order than a request. They followed her into the reception area. A lady sitting at a desk took her name and asked them to take a seat.

Everything looked very old and solid. The desk was inlaid with green leather that matched the thick carpet. The windows were divided across the middle, so that either half could slide up or down. They were open so the warmth could enter but the small room was still cool and damp. The doors leading from the room were made of dark wood and tightly shut. It felt gloomy. It didn't take long before Alfie could feel the gloom creeping into his bones. The musty air smelt horrible. Alfie opened his mouth to breathe, regretting it immediately as the stale air attacked his taste buds.

Relief came as a middle-aged man opened one of the doors and invited them into another room. As Alfie walked in, the fresh air hit his face. He took a couple of deep breaths and the smell eventually left his nostrils. The man was still standing. His trousers didn't quite touch his shoes. Alfie wondered if he had grown recently. A gurgle of laughter entered his throat. He swallowed and looked across at Derek. Clearly, he had spotted the trousers too as his cheeks were sucked in and his face was pink as he tried not to laugh. Alfie quickly looked away. They always found the same things funny but he couldn't risk upsetting Aunt Edith.

'Please take a seat.' The man held out his hand and Aunt Edith sat in a chair close to his desk.

The man rounded the desk and sat down. The glint from the rolled-up golden parchment on top of the desk drew Alfie's attention. The man seemed unwilling to touch it. His hands were clasped together as his fingers fiddled nervously with each other. He cleared his throat and gingerly unrolled the piece of parchment.

'If you would be good enough to read your will before you sign, I'd appreciate it,' he giggled nervously, 'we wouldn't want the parchment to seal it if it was wrong, would we?' His voice rose scarily, ending with a nervous tittering.

Alfie couldn't help himself. He tried to suck in his bottom lip but he started to laugh even though he knew it was rude.

The man looked at him. 'It's really no laughing matter, boy. It's very serious to enter into a contract. It has to be right.'

Alfie didn't know anything about it. He felt his face scrunch up as he spoke, 'It's only paper. Surely you could rip it up.'

'It's Binding Parchment,' said the man, as if that made things clearer.

'Whoever puts their signature on this parchment is bound by the agreement,' explained Aunt Edith. 'The parchment makes sure that it is carried out.'

They both looked very serious, as if lives could depend on it.

'So this parchment is magic,' Alfie realised, 'whatever is written on it actually happens?' He finally understood as they both nodded gravely.

Aunt Edith reached out towards the desk. Her hand hovered over several pens and quills. Alfie watched, fascinated as she lifted a quill, dipped it in an inkwell and gently wiped the tip on the rim before signing the document.

As they left the lawyer's office, Aunt Edith walked slowly as if her joints were stiff. Alfie didn't know many old people. Even though he'd never taken so long to get anywhere, talking to her was fascinating. He watched her crooked body. Her walking stick seemed to have replaced her spine – if he took it away, she would crumble into a heap. *How can that worn out body have such a sharp mind?* As they moved into the sunshine, she seemed to get warmer and walked a little quicker.

'That's better,' she said to herself as she straightened slightly in the sun.

They walked past a large, bright sandstone building. It stood out from the buildings on either side. Aunt Edith slowed down a little.

'That's the museum. You'd probably be interested in some of the things in there.' She nodded towards it.

'Please, no … not the museum,' groaned Derek, worried that they would go inside. Alfie elbowed him gently in the ribs. Luckily she hadn't heard.

'So, what do you think of Wyckerton now?' She smiled at Alfie.

Alfie looked along the street, which was still bustling with activity.

'I…I want to live here forever. It's amazing!' Alfie liked his old village but it couldn't compare to living in a magical city.

'That's thanks to Martyn,' Aunt Edith replied.

Alfie frowned. 'What do you mean? I don't know a Martyn.'

'It's a long story. Have you time to listen?' she asked.

'Yes.' Alfie answered before he looked at Derek, his body had sagged, showing that he'd heard it all before.

Aunt Edith took a deep breath before she spoke, 'Legend tells of two brothers, the most powerful wizards to have ever lived. Martyn, who was loved and respected by all, stood for nobility and justice. His younger brother, Mervyn, stood for evil and deception. As children they were happy. As they grew older, Mervyn started seeking power and wanted to rule over all wizards. The only thing that stood in his way was Martyn. A rift formed between them. Mervyn knew that if he could kill Martyn, all other wizards would bow to him in fear. When Mervyn heard of an object that killed instantly on touch, he spent many years searching for it. They say he located it and gave it to his brother as an anonymous gift, but

Martyn's wife, Ada, found it first. She thought it was for her. As soon as her fingers brushed over the object's surface, her young life left her. Martyn found her dead but without any wounds at all. He knew who had caused it.' She paused to catch her breath.

'What happened next?' Alfie didn't want her to stop.

Aunt Edith shook her head slowly, her eyebrows were drawn together. 'A terrible battle ensued between them, Martyn against Mervyn, good against evil. It was horrific; both equally matched and determined to defeat the other. Martyn eventually whittled Mervyn down but was still incapable of killing him outright. He entombed him somewhere lost to history. If Mervyn had won, he would have ruled over all wizards and would have enjoyed making Martyn's beloved city succumb to dark magic.'

'That's horrible.' Alfie couldn't imagine brothers hating each other so much.

'I know, but at least Martyn managed to save Wyckerton.'

'Did they find the object?'

'Not according to the legend.' Aunt Edith's chin wrinkled. 'Some of Mervyn's possessions are in the museum, though.'

Alfie looked back towards the bright building. Maybe he'd go there sometime.

'That's who Nigel reminds me of,' said Aunt Edith quietly.

'Mervyn!' shouted Alfie, horrified.

'No – Martyn.' Aunt Edith laughed. 'Nigel's as concerned about people's health and happiness as Martyn was. They're both noble men.'

Derek shouted, 'WATCH OUT!'

Alfie spun around and watched as Derek ducked. Three brooms, ridden by children, whizzed over their heads.

They narrowly missed Aunt Edith, who tutted loudly. 'Silly children.'

Alfie was amazed at their speed. 'What are they doing?' he asked.

'Probably playing Manhunt!' said Derek, looking enviously after them.

'What's that?'

'A predator has to tag prey. Last one caught, wins,' explained Derek.

'Same as we play at school,' stated Alfie.

'Same rules but much more exciting! DUCK!' he shouted again.

Alfie watched as another broom hurtled past. He couldn't understand how the rider stayed on.

'Come on. Let's go and see what else we can find to do,' said Derek.

Alfie turned to see if Aunt Edith was all right.

She smiled at him. 'You go. It's not far to the B&B. I'll be fine.'

Alfie ran after Derek who pointed and murmured at the lampposts as they walked past, turning each one a different colour. At the end of the street, they looked back to admire his work.

'At least we'll be able to find our way home,' said Alfie, laughing.

'You have a go.'

Alfie shrugged and shook his head, refusing to try.

'Go on. It's really easy,' Derek insisted.

'I don't want to,' said Alfie. 'I'm not ready.' He didn't know when he would be ready but today didn't seem right.

'Alright.' Derek knew not to push him. It was impossible to change his mind. 'Let's go back to the park,' he said and crossed the road.

The streets were even busier with people enjoying the city at night. Tables and chairs filled up at restaurants offering supper. Alfie watched as a couple approached a restaurant. He could see that there weren't any free tables. Then one appeared from nowhere and they sat down. A notepad hovered, the couple spoke and a quill wrote down their order. The note floated off towards the kitchen. Alfie stood watching in amazement.

Alfie spotted Derek as he disappeared through the tall iron gates leading to the park and ran to catch him. He watched as Derek magically opened and closed flower heads, changed all the lamps from white to colour and attempted to freeze a small fountain.

He huffed when it didn't happen. 'That's a tricky spell, but I'll master it one day!'

Eventually Alfie's stomach started to moan. 'I'm hungry,' he said, 'we'd better get back. I hope we're not late for supper.' Alfie didn't fancy upsetting Mrs Bodley.

'The brilliant thing about you being here is that we can explore again tomorrow evening,' said Derek as they walked back to the B&B.

'I'm still a bit stunned by everything,' admitted Alfie. 'But I'm always up for exploring!'

Back at the B&B, Alfie looked at the sign above the door that said *Park Your Broomstick - Exclusive Bed and Breakfast - Vacancies*. Seeing the name again made him want to laugh aloud. Earlier it had also read *No Vacancies*. The B&B was huge and not full but they didn't want any non-magics knocking at the door during the day. He nodded to himself. *Sensible really.*

*

With his stomach full after supper, Alfie slumped on a huge sofa in the sitting room. The day of discovery had tired him. Aunt Edith was napping as usual. He decided to go upstairs and find Derek. When he arrived at the top of the stone staircase, he stopped. He could hear chatting along the corridor and decided to investigate. He peeped into Pippa and Fizz's room as Mrs Bodley put them to bed. He felt a fleeting moment of envy. He couldn't remember moments like these with his mother.

'But why do we have to go to bed. It's not even dark yet…' Pippa's brows were drawn together. She was seven and didn't agree with her bedtime.

Fizz joined in even though she could hardly keep her eyes open. 'We're not tired…' she said, but her voice trailed off as she concentrated on sitting up.

Mrs Bodley kissed them both. 'Just lay your heads down on your pillows. Then we'll discuss what would be a good bedtime.' She seemed very relaxed. Both slid down into their beds.

'Sleep tight,' she whispered and winked at Alfie. The girls' eyes shut immediately. They were both asleep within seconds.

Alfie's mouth opened wide in disbelief. 'How did you do that?'

'I've put a charm on their pillows,' she smiled and raised her shoulders gently as if she had been naughty, 'it just needs the prompt of *sleep tight*. I don't want them to sleep if they lie on their beds during the day.'

Alfie looked at her warily.

'Don't worry, you're too old for tricks.' She reassured him. He wasn't convinced.

Derek met him on the landing. 'I was just coming to find you. I've been thinking…'

'Did it hurt?' Alfie knew it was a bad joke but he couldn't help sniggering as they walked back into their bedroom.

Derek shook his head and crossed his eyes. 'I was thinking about magic. I don't really know how to help you learn any. I started so young I don't remember not being able to do it. I wouldn't know where to start.' He seemed at a loss, as if he was letting Alfie down.

'It's okay. When I'm used to the idea that I'm magic, I'm sure it will just happen. You said I magically did those things before and I wasn't even trying.' Alfie found it hard to believe that he'd done them. He hadn't done anything since.

They were both worn out from the excitement of the past few days. Alfie decided to have an early night. After he'd showered, he went back into the bedroom.

Derek was lying on his bed, reading. 'All that walking has worn me out.' Derek's voice was weary.

'Me too.' Alfie decided to see if Mrs Bodley had been telling the truth. 'Sleep tight,' he said.

Derek's head shot off the pillow. 'What?' he said in disbelief. 'You sound like my Mum. She hasn't said that for ages.' He thumped his head back down and carried on reading.

Alfie was relieved that their pillows weren't charmed but as soon as his head rested on his, he felt his eyes grow heavy. Within seconds he fell asleep.

CHAPTER SIX

F.L.U.C.E.R. it

ALFIE had been in Wyckerton just over a week. He was about to enter the kitchen when Mrs Bodley bustled past him. He realised that some of the excuses Derek had used were true. Mrs Bodley was always busy.

'Shall I walk Ernie?' he asked, wanting to be helpful.

'That would be a good idea. Thank you,' responded Mrs Bodley, smiling at him.

'Why don't you have someone to help you?' he asked.

Mrs Bodley looked surprised. 'Why?'

'You seem to work hard.'

'This isn't hard work. I choose what I want to do,' she said.

'And for the rest you use magic?' asked Alfie.

'No,' she whispered, and held her finger up to her lips. 'Shh – I ask Mr Bodley to do it.'

Alfie smiled and took Ernie's lead down from its hook. He tried to latch it to Ernie's collar. As he slipped his fingers behind it to get a better grip, he was surprised how tiny Ernie's neck felt. Ernie immediately rolled on his back, twisting Alfie's fingers in the collar. He struggled to untangle them as Ernie started to chew the lead with his needle-like teeth.

'Come on, Ernie. If you don't put this on, you can't go out.' Alfie grabbed the collar again and tried to attach the lead. He started to laugh as Ernie rolled around and brought his feet into the battle, his fat little paws pushing Alfie away. Eventually Alfie secured the lead but he couldn't get him to walk. Every time Ernie felt the tug of the lead, he changed direction to try and outwit it.

'He always does that.' Mr Bodley had watched the show, smiling. 'He will give in eventually. Then he's quite good at heeling.'

Alfie nodded.

Mr Bodley leant to whisper, 'I heard what Mrs Bodley said. Don't tell her, but *I* use magic for the jobs she gives me. Mum's the word.' He winked.

Alfie smiled. Mr Bodley had the same sense of humour as Derek.

Alfie and Ernie strolled along the paths and played on the grass. It was before six o'clock and Wyckerton seemed like an ordinary city. He saw another dog being walked. It was also a German Shepherd but was fully-grown. Its coat was completely black and very glossy. Ernie's fur was more like wool. It couldn't be separated so that his skin showed through. Alfie had tried to groom him but it was impossible. When the brush wasn't stuck in his fur, it was being attacked and chewed by his sharp teeth.

'Right. That's long enough, I think. Come on, Ernie let's go back to the B&B.'

Ernie had other ideas. On their way back, he tugged on his lead wanting to go along the side passage of a shop. Alfie tried to stop him but Ernie pulled the lead tight. He turned around so that he was facing Alfie and wriggled his head from side to side, determined to go where he wanted. His collar had come up behind his ears. Alfie gave in, worried that he would hurt himself. They went into the garden.

Alfie heard a noise in a room that opened onto the garden. He followed Ernie towards it, not knowing what to expect. He looked in through the open door and saw the tidiest workshop he had ever seen. The tools were set out on the end wall. Each one shadowed a drawing so that, if it was used, its empty place could easily be spotted. Screwdrivers, several hammers of various sizes, the sharpest, shiniest axe imaginable and some odd-looking tools hung in rows. A handmade bench stretched down one wall. A cauldron sat in the centre of the bench but his gaze moved to the black cat curled up at the end.

Alfie jumped as a man looked up. He was sitting on a stool by the bench doing paperwork.

'Hello.' The man seemed busy until he saw the puppy. 'Ernie, come here, boy, I'm sure I can find you a treat.'

Ernie pulled on his lead forcing Alfie to go into the room. The man stroked Ernie. Alfie felt awkward until he remembered that they'd met outside the B&B.

'You're Nigel, aren't you?' said Alfie. 'I've never seen such a neat workshop.'

'Thank you. I took over when my father died. Most of the tools have been passed down through the generations.' He looked at them. 'I doubt whether some are still made nowadays.'

'That axe looks brand new,' said Alfie.

'It isn't. It's an odd axe though. Always seems to cut best on the second swing.'

Because Alfie didn't understand what he meant, he changed the subject. 'Do you live here?'

'Yes, my wife, Mary, and I do. Above the shop.'

Now that Alfie was inside the room he could see the last wall. It was lined with shelves packed with blue bottles of various sizes, the glass almost too dark to see through. One shelf was stacked high with small, empty vials. A huge jar was filled with cork stoppers for the vials.

'Oh, I remember. Aunt Edith said you run a potion shop.'

'That's right,' said Nigel. 'It seems to be something I'm quite good at. It's rather fun.'

'She said you were the best potion-maker in Wyckerton!' Alfie blurted out.

Nigel chuckled. 'That was kind.'

Alfie perched on the edge of the bench. 'What does "FLUCER it" mean?'

Nigel frowned at Alfie who pointed at a sign stuck up on a roof beam. Nigel looked towards the sign.

'Oh, that. My father made that sign when it was his workshop. It means...' he listed the letters individually with their explanation.

Find it
Look at it
Use it
Clean it
Examine it
Return it.

'See, F.L.U.C.E.R it.' Nigel smiled at the memory of his father. 'His brothers borrowed his tools. If they bothered to return them, they would always be dirty or broken.'

'Hopefully the sign worked.' Alfie thought that he would be angry if someone borrowed something and didn't look after it.

'Hopefully it did,' said Nigel.

'Watch this. Ernie can do a trick.' Alfie jumped down from the bench and took a treat out of his pocket. He knelt down and held his hands behind his back.

Ernie immediately came and sat opposite him. Alfie brought both fists around in front of him. 'Which hand?' he challenged Ernie, who lifted a paw and placed it carefully on Alfie's left hand. 'Clever boy!' he said as he turned his hand over to reveal the treat.

'Did you have one in each hand?' asked Nigel.

'No, look.' Alfie opened the other hand. 'I'll do it again and change hands.' He did and Ernie chose correctly. 'He even gets it right if you don't swap,' he said proudly.

Nigel looked at Ernie. 'Well, aren't you clever?' His brows drew together, 'and you're actually quite odd-looking at the moment?' He hadn't seen Ernie for a while.

Alfie saw Ernie everyday and hadn't noticed him change. He examined him carefully. He was a strange mixture of puppy and dog. He no longer had cute puppy ears. They were now upright, but collected together in the middle and leaned slightly to one side. His puppy nose had gone and was replaced by a long grown-up one. The fur running back to his ears was glossy and no longer woolly like the rest of him. Unnoticed, he had become an adolescent.

Ernie started to rumble. Alfie laughed as he realised it was a growl. It turned into a yap as a shadow appeared at the door.

'Hello Nigel. I'm trying to make a gargoyle potion but I can't seem to get it right. I've heard you've managed one or two, even with your busy schedule.' The slimy voice mocked.

Alfie watched as Nigel stiffened. Ernie continued to rumble.

'I'd rather you didn't use the back door, Damian. Use the shop entrance,' said Nigel. 'I haven't made that potion for ages. Let me think.'

The man ignored Alfie. Alfie scrutinised him from top to toe. He didn't like what he saw. Greasy red hair flicked out wildly where it wasn't stuck to his head. Stains covered his cloak like a world map and his shoes were covered with dirt. His face and hands were white, as if they had never seen the sun.

'I'll have to write it down for you.' Nigel tried to find a blank piece of paper on the bench. 'Let me get some paper,' he said as he left the room.

Alfie bent down to stroke Ernie and watched as Damian moved to the pile of papers. He slid one over the other as he quickly read them.

Alfie felt as if he were invisible.

Damian pushed the papers together and stepped away from them as Nigel walked back into the room. Nigel wasn't fooled. He pushed the paperwork into a drawer as he sat down and started to write.

'There you go,' Nigel said as he handed Damian the paper. 'It's not a difficult potion, after all.'

'Perhaps not for you. Luck, I presume.' Damian sneered as he left.

'Horrible man,' said Nigel aloud. 'Sorry. That was rude.'

'He didn't look that pleasant,' said Alfie, glad he had left.

'No.' Nigel smiled. 'I guess he's at a loose end while his wife and son are away looking after her ill mother.'

Alfie wrinkled his nose. 'He's someone's father?' *Poor them!*

'His son, Odii, is as bad!' Nigel chuckled. 'Don't feel sorry for him!'

Alfie didn't anymore. He hoped he'd never meet him.

'Damian has a potion shop in the Northeast Quarter but he's not that good at making them. I don't know how he makes a living.'

'He was going through your papers.'

'I'm used to that. He wants my potion recipes.'

'Why do you help him?'

'Everyone deserves a chance. I see it as my duty to try and keep his customers safe.'

'They should come to you, then they wouldn't have to worry.'

'Thank you.' Nigel smiled. 'You've been in Wyckerton a while now. How are you enjoying living here?'

'It's brilliant, but I haven't done any magic yet.'

Secretly, Alfie had tried to make a pencil move but he had concentrated so much it hurt his brain and his eyes had started to sting from lack of blinking.

'Well, I reckon I could give you some pointers.' Nigel's kind face had taken on a warm glow.

Alfie couldn't believe it, his brows shot up to meet his hair. 'Really?'

'I might not be the world's greatest wizard, but I could certainly get you started.' Nigel looked at Alfie as if he really wanted to help.

Crikey, it would be great to have lessons. 'That would be fantastic,' he said.

Nigel's face nearly split in half, his grin was so wide it was infectious.

Alfie grinned back. 'When can we start?' he asked.

'How about Saturdays? We could start the week after next. I'll teach you when we're not busy. In return, you could help me make potions here in the workshop. Or if Mary gets busy with customers, you could help in our shop.' Nigel seemed to like the idea more and more. 'Or would you prefer to deliver potions after six?'

'I'd like to do all of it!' Alfie held out his hand. 'Agreed,' he said as they shook hands.

Alfie almost bounced on the way back to the B&B. Ernie trotted along beside him as he wondered if he had mini bouncy castles on his feet instead of shoes.

He couldn't stop grinning. Meeting Nigel again today had been a stroke of luck. Alfie needed a mentor and Nigel made him feel comfortable about magic. It was as if Nigel was to Alfie what Wyckerton was to wizards. Alfie had found his destiny.

Derek was in the sitting room. Alfie flopped down into the plump cushion beside him.

He told Derek about Nigel. 'I can't wait, but I'm worried that I'll be useless,' he admitted.

Derek seemed positive. 'It's brilliant that Nigel's going to help you, though. He'll be really good. You'll be doing spells before you know it.'

'Mm, maybe.' Alfie wasn't sure but he knew that Derek always considered everything. 'You're probably right.'

'I'm sure you'll be fine when you get used to the idea that you're magic,' said Derek.

Alfie looked across at him and wondered if he had any idea how strange that sentence sounded.

*

Alfie soon settled into life in Wyckerton. He and Derek had a routine, which involved playing with Ernie during the day and exploring during the evening.

'It's really different having you here. It's like having a brother,' said Derek.

'I feel like that, too,' said Alfie.

'Fancy exploring the castle ruins tomorrow…?'

Before Alfie could answer, Mrs Bodley bustled into their room. 'I don't want you going there,' she said sternly. 'Can you tidy your room, please? I want to clean it and you've left things all over the place.' She was looking at both of them as she spoke. 'You know what will happen if I move anything. You'll moan for days that you can't find it.'

Alfie wanted to argue but, as he looked around the room, he had to admit that it was difficult to find any space on the floor.

'Okay, but can you give us some time?' Derek tried to bargain, hoping that she would forget to come back.

'No. It needs to be done in the next ten minutes,' she looked at her watch, 'starting...now!' She didn't look back as she left but they could see her heading for the girls' room. They knew she meant it.

They started picking up their own clothes and slinging them in drawers and any spaces that were out of sight. Alfie was pleased to have the trunk at the end of his bed. He slung his stuff into it and finished first.

He offered to help Derek. 'Where do you want me to put these?' He was holding sweets and biscuits.

'Oh, they can go in my trunk. Mum will go mad if she sees that I've brought them up here.' Derek didn't look as concerned as he sounded.

Alfie bunged them in the trunk along with anything else of Derek's that he could find.

'That looks good to me...' he said as he looked around the room. He shut the lid of the trunk and started to close the latch.

'Don't lock...it.' Derek realised he was too late.

Alfie tried to stop the latch clicking but couldn't release the pressure in time. 'Why?'

'I put a charm on it to make the lock harder to open. I'm sure the girls nose around in my stuff. I've forgotten what it is, though.' Derek shook his head, as if silently scolding himself for being an idiot.

'You'll remember it soon.'

'Don't expect so. It was months ago and I haven't a clue what it is. I'll just have to sneak up more biscuits.' Derek's smile was wonky. Alfie knew it would quickly disappear if Mrs Bodley were within earshot.

Alfie took a deep breath, *Oh no...* 'I also put your cloak in there...' he admitted slowly.

Derek looked fed up. 'Oh dregs!' he said and sighed.

Mrs Bodley came back into the room and looked around. 'Well, that looks better,' she said. 'At least you know where everything is.'

She smiled and whooshed her arm over the room so that it dusted and cleaned itself. *No vacuum cleaners needed here.*

'Bed early tonight. You have school in the morning,' she said as she left the room.

Neither of them heard her parting comment. They were still thinking about Derek's trunk.

Alfie looked around the room and liked how big it was. The board games were back in their boxes. Derek's collection of model trains were neatly placed on top of the dresser. They definitely knew where everything was, even Derek's cloak, which was now locked away in the wrong place.

'My Dad's left me some money for essentials. Can I buy a cloak?' Alfie looked at Derek. 'The walk might help you remember how to undo the charm on your trunk,' he added hopefully.

'Doubt it, but I don't mind coming with you. We could go tomorrow after six.'

Alfie's grin grew until his face hurt. Tomorrow, he would own a real wizard cloak.

CHAPTER SEVEN

School

'UP you get. You have school today,' said Mrs Bodley as she opened the curtains.

'School? But we've left school,' Alfie was still half-asleep. He didn't want to be awake if he had to go to school.

'Only primary school. You need an education so that you can get a job and live among non-magics later if you want to,' she answered and left the room to wake the girls.

'School…' moaned Alfie. 'I thought being magic meant we were through with all that.'

'It doesn't work like that…' Derek's voice was groggy.

Getting washed and dressed on a school day was much more difficult than during the holidays. Alfie looked in the bathroom mirror. He stuck his tongue out hoping it would be orange with green spots so that he could have the day off. Annoyingly, it looked perfectly normal.

Mrs Bodley was leaving the bedroom as he walked out of the bathroom. 'I've placed your new uniform on your bed.' She smiled gently as if she guessed he would be sad.

'Thank you.' Alfie sighed gratefully. He would have missed his father too much if he had gone shopping for it without him. When they were dressed, they went down for breakfast. Alfie's nostrils twitched at the smell of bacon and eggs. It was even more tempting on a school day.

Some of the guests wore their cloaks as they sat at the enchanted table. It was safe within the B&B.

Mr Bodley looked up and smiled. 'Ah, there you are,' he said, while chomping away at his breakfast. 'I just wanted to remind you that the school has many non-magics who are teachers and pupils. Remember to hide the magic until the bell tolls!'

Alfie sat down. He ran his finger around his new shirt collar, trying to make it more comfortable as he wondered how Mr Bodley could be so cheerful on a school morning. Then he realised it was because he didn't have to go.

'I still can't do any yet.' Alfie's brows drew together, anxious that going to school would set him back further with his magic. Maybe he should mention it to Mrs Bodley.

Derek looked up. 'But you soon will be able to…'

Alfie nodded. He hoped that Derek was right. Pleasure sparked in his chest as he remembered Nigel's promised lessons.

Alfie hadn't ever paid much attention to the school when he'd played with Derek in the city. He knew where it was and was sure that Mrs Bodley sent them on their way far too early. It turned out that she knew what she was doing. Each footstep moved them forward only half the distance that it would have on a non-school day.

Alfie dragged his feet. Why was the warm September sun plotting against him? He wanted to be in the park with Ernie on a day like this.

They arrived at the huge Victorian school building before they needed to be there. It was barely eight o'clock but the entrance gates were open. They followed the other pupils to the front door.

Alfie walked through the entrance porch and into a small hall. Passages led off to each side. Stone mullions punctured the red brick wall in front of him, forming an enormous arch. He moved forward through the arch and went down two steps into the main hall. The dimness seemed worse after the bright autumn sunlight. He stood with Derek, unsure where to go. The other children were heading in various directions. He wondered how they knew where they were going.

It was a relief when a lady approached them. 'Welcome. I'm the school secretary, Miss Fenshaw. Is it your first day?' she asked.

Derek answered, 'Yes.'

'Right. If you could tell me your names, I can mark you off my sheet and explain where you should go.' Her mouth smiled but it didn't reach her eyes. Her glasses were perched on the end of her nose and she peered over the rims. Alfie supressed a grin. She resembled an *actual* secretary bird – all thin and bossy.

Alfie didn't dare look at Derek. He would have spotted it too, which would set them both off laughing.

Miss Fenshaw looked at him with one eyebrow raised as if he was peculiar.

'I'm Derek Bodley...' said Derek obediently.

'And I'm Alfie Walters.'

'Good.' She found their names on her list and ticked them. Every movement she made was twitchy and sharp, as if she were a clockwork doll. 'Now, you need to go to the assembly hall. If you go through that door,' she turned the top half of her body and pointed, 'you'll find a board on the wall with a map of the school.'

She looked down her nose, gave them another fake smile and walked off.

Derek led the way to the huge notice board that was at the entrance of the staff room. 'So... it tells us on here where we're supposed to go,' Derek looked from it to Alfie and back again. He pulled a face before he spotted something, 'Ah, there look. The assembly hall. I need to find where we are now...' His voice was so quiet he was almost talking to himself.

A passing older boy butted in, 'It's through here.'

'Thank you.'

The boy had already disappeared.

They finally found the assembly hall and squeezed past some other pupils until they could see a teacher standing at the front. They sat down.

Eventually the teacher spoke, 'Good morning, I am Mr Adams. I am the headmaster.' He strung his words out with perfect pronunciation. He was short and his hair had divided and slipped down either side of his head so that it sat just above his ears, leaving a huge bald patch. He seemed pleased that he was so important.

But I bet you're not magic, Alfie thought as he swallowed a chuckle.

'Right. On the wall at the back of the hall, you will find a list. There is also a plan showing the layout of the classrooms. Find your name and note which classroom you need to go to.' Mr Adams rolled each "R" slowly, making the speech last longer. He seemed to like the sound of his own voice.

Alfie looked around when he heard chatting. He spotted a kind-looking older teacher explaining something to a younger one. His face was expressive and his hands were flailing around as he talked. He puffed himself up before he exploded into laughter. The younger man glanced at Mr Adams and looked slightly self-conscious. Alfie continued to look around at the other children. He did a double-take as he noticed a lady with a very white face. She looked like a ghost. Her expression was annoyed as she glared at the older teacher, making it clear that she disapproved of talking.

'Any problems, ask one of the teachers who will be only too happy to help.' Mr Adams was still talking.

Alfie's gaze fell on a spindly teacher, her straight hair looked like an upside-down bowl. She seemed appalled at the thought of being approached by several children. Alfie glanced back to the cheerful man hoping that he would be his teacher.

'Let's roam over there and read the list!' said Derek, rolling each "R" in perfect imitation of Mr Adams.

Alfie desperately tried to think of a sentence with an "R" in it, 'Absolutely!' he said and they both giggled at his pathetic attempt.

Alfie was pleased that the list of names showed that he was in the same form room as Derek. They checked the classroom plan. Once they had seen the system for room numbers, it all made sense. Blocks were A to D and started at the back of the main building from the left.

They set off, confident of finding the correct room. They soon realised that the route they had chosen was a long one. The paths twisted and turned instead of going directly there. It took ages to get to the area they needed. Eventually they came to the buildings that were separate from the main structure. They were built of the same red brick as the old building but were much newer. The window frames were made from timber instead of stone and metal. Without the layout plan in front of them, they didn't have a clue which one they were supposed to enter. They peered into a room through the clear glass window.

'There must be loads of pupils at this school,' Alfie commented, 'all of these rooms are classrooms.'

'I suppose a lot of pupils come from outside the city,' said Derek. 'We'd better hurry. We don't want to be late.'

They found their classroom. Alfie sat down at a desk next to Derek. The hugeness of the school hit him. At primary school they'd stayed in the same room with the same teacher. They'd only moved classrooms for special subjects like art and sport.

By the time everyone had arrived about thirty pupils were in the room. Derek nodded at two boys as they walked past. They were both taller than Alfie and Derek. One of them could have been an adult.

Derek leant towards Alfie and whispered, 'They're Bun and Chris. The ones I told you about – from the city.'

Alfie nodded and looked at them. He was surprised that they didn't look any different from anyone else, until he realised that neither did he or Derek. They were all wearing the school uniform, dark grey trousers and jumper, white shirt with a red and grey striped tie.

Alfie leant towards Derek and whispered, 'There are a lot of non-magics.'

Derek frowned at him, 'Shh, that's why we have to be careful!'

Alfie recognised their form teacher. He was the younger teacher who had been talking to the cheerful, older one in the assembly hall. He was dressed completely in brown.

'Good Morning, I'm Mr Watts,' he said. As he passed around exercise books he explained how the school day would run.

Alfie realised that he hadn't been listening. He shook his head.

This is important. He shouldn't always rely on Derek to tell him what was going on.

'You need to copy your timetable from the board onto the form in the front of your school diary. Make sure you double-check the room for each lesson *before* you write it down, otherwise you'll be running around the school even more than you need to.' Mr Watts seemed pleasant, not too old and quite friendly. Alfie hoped the other teachers were like him.

'Sir, some of the spaces don't have room numbers,' one of the girls pointed out.

Mr Watts smiled reassuringly. 'Those are the ones where you're in sets. When you've finished copying the timetable, come and see me individually. I'll tell you which room numbers you need to write down.'

Everyone started to stand up. Alfie looked down at his diary. He'd only filled out half of Monday. How had they all finished so quickly?

'So you're quick writers?' Mr Watts took control. 'Everyone, sit down. We'll start with this row,' he indicated a line of desks, 'if you haven't finished when it's your turn, I'll come back to you.'

Thank goodness. Alfie blew his hair away from his eyes. He tried to write quickly, grateful that most of the lessons were doubles and that all of Wednesday afternoon was sports.

'Don't worry,' whispered Derek, 'you can copy mine later.'

Alfie smiled at him but was determined to do it himself.

By the time Derek had spoken to Mr Watts, Alfie had managed to scribble out all he needed. He made his way up to Mr Watts' desk to find out his set. When he sat down again, he checked with Derek. They had every lesson together. *Brilliant.*

The end of lesson bell pierced through the air, making Alfie jump.

'Right. You have all the information you need. Check which room you're in next. Make your way there, please. I'll see you back here for register after lunch.' Mr Watts smiled at them as they piled out of the door.

They ended up hurrying to find the correct room.

Alfie looked through his exercise books to find the right one for this lesson and placed it on his desk, its red cover bright against the wood. He looked up as the door swung open forcefully and the spindly teacher from the assembly hall who'd seemed most unwilling to help entered.

'I am Mrs Stott,' she said slowly as she looked at each face individually, pausing for a second on each one, 'and this is a geography lesson. I like geography. I don't want you to spoil that for me. I expect you to try your hardest at all times.'

Alfie swallowed. He felt like Mrs Stott was talking directly to him, as though she knew that he found it hard to concentrate during lessons. Some of the pupils in front of him squirmed in their seats, which made him feel better. He wasn't alone.

By the end of the double lesson, Alfie knew that he didn't like geography. He didn't want to know where anywhere else was or what it was like there because he would stay in Wyckerton forever.

Outside, as the fresh air hit him, he realised that he had hardly breathed all lesson. He gulped in as the cool air soothed his lungs like nectar.

At break-time Derek introduced him to Bun and Chris.

'This is Alfie.'

Alfie nodded at them.

The first boy was a little taller than him, with brown hair and eyes. 'I'm Bun,' he said.

The Persuader. Alfie could see what Derek meant. Somehow Bun made him feel important.

'And I'm Chris.'

Alfie crooked his neck back to see Chris's face. He was way taller than Alfie and at least twice as wide. He would have been scary if his face hadn't been so kind.

'What did you think of the timetable?' squeaked Alfie, he would never normally have spoken to anyone that looked like Chris.

'It's okay,' said Chris, 'lots of sport. Didn't think much of the geography teacher though. Made me feel a bit nervous.'

Alfie had to stop his jaw dropping. How could Chris feel the same as he did?

'We have double English next,' said Bun.

'So have we!' said Derek.

As they discussed their timetables on the way to the English lesson, they found that they shared nearly all lessons during the week. They separated into pairs as they walked into the classroom.

Alfie sat next to Derek and nervously waited for the English teacher to enter the room. The whole class had their green exercise books on their desks. When the teacher came in, they all breathed a sigh of relief. It was the jolly, older teacher that Alfie had liked from the assembly hall. Close up, he looked like a cross between the perfect Grandad and Father Christmas.

'Good Morning, I'm Mr Kalm. I'd like to welcome you all to the school.'

Mr Kalm suited his name. He didn't even seem worried that his cardigan was buttoned wrongly or that his socks didn't match. Alfie understood most of the things Mr Kalm said, even though he couldn't swear that he heard all of them. He relaxed, finding the lesson much easier than geography.

When they left the lesson and headed for the canteen, the food smells made Alfie feel weak. They joined the long, slow queue. Alfie grabbed a tray and started to pile it up with everything he liked. He even popped some wrapped biscuits into his pocket. He followed Derek and they sat at an empty table.

As he ate he noticed Bun and Chris join the queue. 'We'll be finished by the time they get through.'

'Not if I know Bun,' said Derek.

A dinner lady, her brow furrowed, looked down the line before she smiled and signalled for Bun and Chris to come to the front of the queue. An older boy challenged them as they walked past but Bun said something and he let them carry on. The dinner lady filled two trays with food and handed them to Bun and Chris while they waited.

'How did you manage that?' asked Alfie as Bun and Chris joined them.

'We helped her carry boxes of food into the kitchen this morning,' said Bun.

Chris finished his food in a few mouthfuls.

'Come on, let's go and explore!' said Bun, when he'd finished eating.

They emptied their trays, went outside and walked around the grounds of the school. Chris wandered off to talk to two girls, then re-joined them as they walked around the boundary of the sports field. Now they knew that Alfie lived in the city, they were trying to keep away from the non-magics so they wouldn't be overheard.

'I just spoke to the Robin Hoods,' said Chris.

'Who are they?' asked Alfie.

'Two girls from the city,' answered Chris, 'but instead of robbing the rich to feed the poor, they protect the weak from bullies.'

'How?'

'All sorts of ways. You'll probably see for yourself soon,' said Chris.

'What are they really called?' asked Alfie.

'Martha and Jazz.'

Odd name. 'Jazz…' he said aloud.

'Jasmine, I think,' said Chris.

'She knows everything about music,' said Bun as they continued to walk. 'Do you want to meet up after school?'

'We can't. We're going to get Alfie a cloak. He hasn't had one before,' explained Derek.

Bun smiled as if he knew how important it was. 'That's good. Derek will make sure you buy a good one,' said Bun.

Alfie agreed. He knew Derek wouldn't let him down. He'd even made it easier finding out that he was magic.

'Maybe we could all meet in the park another evening?' said Chris.

Alfie listened excitedly. He liked having more friends, especially magic ones. He wasn't even worried that he couldn't join in yet.

During the first afternoon class, they managed to sit close together but they were slow getting to the double maths lesson.

When they entered the classroom only two empty tables were left and they were on opposite sides of the room.

'We'll pass notes,' said Bun as they separated to sit down. 'Better find out what the teacher's like first, though,' he said as an afterthought.

Derek nodded towards two girls as he and Alfie sat down. 'They're Martha and Jazz,' he said.

The Robin Hoods. Martha looked delicate, as if she'd break if the wind blew too hard. Her blonde hair was fluffy. Jazz was taller, with short, shiny dark hair. She looked more athletic but was still small.

Alfie looked across at Bun as the door opened and the maths teacher walked in. She stooped to pick up a piece of litter. She carefully placed it in the bin by her desk before she acknowledged that there was anyone else in the room.

She stood very upright, her perfect, platinum blond hair was pulled up into a tight bun and her suit was immaculate. Her face was ghostly white. Alfie knew that maths wouldn't be fun.

'I'm Miss Lloyd,' she said sternly. 'Mathematics is an orderly subject. It has a purpose and always has a correct answer. It's my job to make sure you succeed at finding it.'

Alfie looked down at the book on his desk and wondered if the colour went with the teacher on purpose. Miss Lloyd and the cold, ice blue cover were certainly a perfect match. He couldn't help checking that his tie was straight.

'I have written some maths problems on the board. I would like you to complete them so that I can assess your individual abilities.' She turned to the board and started to rewrite some that were smudged.

Alfie looked across at Bun to see if they dared to pass notes. Bun shrugged, undecided.

'Put that sweet away, Edward.' said Miss Lloyd, without turning around.

Alfie looked towards the boy in trouble. He had been about to put a sweet in his mouth. Alfie sighed loudly as he saw Edward and then John, who was sitting next to him. It hadn't occurred to Alfie that the bullies he had caught stealing money at primary school would be in his class.

'How did you know my name?' asked Edward.

'I know all of your names,' replied Miss Lloyd, still writing.

Derek nudged Alfie and nodded towards Bun. He was shaking his head to say that they wouldn't be writing notes.

'Even Bun won't be able to play mind games with her,' whispered Derek.

Alfie didn't answer. He didn't want Edward to notice him.

As they left the room at the end of the lesson, Alfie said, 'I wish we weren't in the same class as Edward and John.'

'Me, too. Maybe they've changed?' Derek looked hopeful.

'Bullies never change.'

Alfie's mood took a definite upturn, though, when Chris said, 'Bullies, eh. I expect Martha and Jazz will deal with them.'

*

It was a relief when the first day was over. As they walked home, Alfie learnt about Bun and Chris. They had both lived in Wyckerton all their lives. They'd gone to their local primary school, which was why Alfie had never met them. He was pleased that all the pupils were brought together at senior school.

'I've moved into Derek's B&B. I used to live in a village outside Wyckerton,' said Alfie.

Bun and Chris glanced at Derek, confused. Derek nodded to reassure them.

'Loads of people come and go at the B&B,' said Chris and smiled. 'So the cupboards are always full of food.'

'Not after you've been around!' joked Derek. 'I don't know how you're not twenty stone.'

Alfie looked up at Chris, and guessed that everything he ate turned into muscle. 'Well, I hope I'll live at the B&B forever!'

Derek agreed. 'It's fun having you there. We can gang up against my sisters.'

Bun and Chris rolled their eyes skywards as if they knew his sisters only too well. Alfie didn't say that he enjoyed their noise. It was better than the silence of his house.

Alfie remembered his visit to Nigel's shop. 'Do you know Nigel?' he asked.

'Yes,' said Bun.

Chris nodded.

'I'm going to help in his shop. I'm going to deliver potions for him.'

'Wow, that will be good, especially if you can help him make them.' Chris seemed impressed.

Bun slowed down as they arrived at the end of his road. 'Hope you get a good cloak tonight,' he said.

'Thanks. I think I'll walk Ernie before we go though.' Alfie looked at Derek to see if he wanted to come too.

'Is that your puppy?' asked Chris, looking at Derek.

Derek nodded. 'Yes, but he seems to grow every day!'

'That reminds me. Jazz told me about Richard today,' said Chris. 'You know, the antiques dealer?'

Derek and Bun nodded.

'No,' said Alfie.

Derek tried to be helpful. 'His shop is called Slightly Shabby...' Alfie shrugged his shoulders.

'He's Nigel's friend,' said Derek, as if that explained everything and turned back to Chris.

Chris continued, 'Well, his dog died.'

'Aw, that's sad,' said Alfie.

'Yes, but that's only half the story. He was walking down by the river in the park and they both just fell over. Richard was so shocked he took a while to stand up. His dog died, but no one knows how.'

'Was he old?' asked Bun.

'About sixty, I think,' said Chris.

'No! Not Richard. The dog?'

'Oh. It was only two,' Chris corrected himself.

Derek looked confused. 'This sounds like a mystery for you,

Alfie. Maybe you could help Richard find out what happened to his dog.'

'There doesn't seem to be much to go on,' responded Alfie.

'See you tomorrow,' said Chris as they separated to go home.

They walked into the B&B. Alfie was relieved to see that Ernie was alive and well. He gave him an extra large fuss. He took Ernie on a long walk but on the way back to the B&B he hurried, excited about buying his first cloak.

CHAPTER EIGHT

The Burglary

ALFIE and Derek strolled along the busy street as office workers, school children and a few tourists milled about on their way home. The number of people in the city during the day always amazed Alfie.

'I told you we'd be early,' moaned Derek as they arrived at the cloak shop.

'I didn't know it was this close,' said Alfie as he looked through the window. 'I'd like to go in anyway.'

Derek turned to him with a look of horror on his face. 'It's a ladies clothes shop!' He stated as if Alfie hadn't realised.

'I know, but I've never seen a shop change from the inside.'

'But it's a clothes shop,' Derek said again. 'There are women in there!'

'Come on!' ordered Alfie.

They pretended to look at the items for sale. Alfie noted the bored expression on Derek's face but he didn't care. Today was an exception. He hid behind a pillar as a lady paid for her items. As she went towards the door, she paused to look at something else.

Alfie groaned to himself, *Please just leave and hurry home.* He jutted his chin forward trying to push her on her way. A noise made him look towards Derek. He was behind a clothes rail with his arms slipped into the sleeves of a huge, white shirt. He flapped them about and made ghost noises behind her. Alfie smiled. She didn't notice Derek as she left the shop. They came out of their hiding places.

Alfie fidgeted as they waited. Time seemed to have slowed down. Then it happened… One, two … as the third chime became an echo, the shop started to change from a mundane clothes shop.

The walls of shelves that were filled with neatly folded garments changed from bright everyday colours into magical wizard-wear in shades of deep-sea blues, moss greens and plum reds. Rich colours that would proudly adorn their wearers.

Alfie jumped when the shopkeeper spoke.

'How can I help you?' She was now wearing an outfit worthy of her heritage. Her emerald green cloak looked heavy.

'Um, I'd like to buy a cloak, please.' Alfie put his hand in his pocket and felt the money his father had left for him to spend. He held the notes firmly in his fist. It had been burning a hole in his pocket since the day he'd found out that he was magic but he hadn't had the courage to dress like a wizard.

'Colour preference?' asked the assistant.

'Do you have a dark coloured one that reflects the light?' Alfie felt embarrassed that he cared.

'I believe I do,' she smiled knowingly, 'that's a popular choice for younger wizards.' She moved off to find one.

Alfie couldn't move. He'd been recognised as a wizard. A little laugh bubbled up and escaped. The assistant came back with a dark-maroon coloured cloak. He took it from her. The material felt heavy and thick in his hand. The weight surprised him. He swung it around his shoulders. It fitted perfectly. He turned to look in the mirror and watched as the light moved over the cloth. He was mesmerised as he slowly moved his arms, the changing colours flowed down them like liquid.

He tried to squash the slight niggle which made him wonder if he should buy a bigger one, "with room to grow" as his father would always say. He tugged the cloak closer. He really wanted this one. It felt right.

'This one is from our Distend range. It's a Distend Slim, with no trimmings. I thought you would prefer a plain one. Of course it will grow with you, so you'll only have to replace it if you wear it out or want a different colour,' said the assistant helpfully.

Alfie couldn't believe it. 'Really?' he asked, his voice slightly higher pitched than normal.

She smiled at him. 'It's from the middle range, cost-wise. Would you like to try one from a different collection?'

'No, thank you. I'll take this one.' He took the money out of his pocket and willingly handed it to her. This was the best present he had ever had.

'Do you want to wear it or shall I put it in a bag?'

He looked at Derek. 'I'd like it in a bag, please.'

She packed it and handed it to him.

'How do some wizards change into their cloaks as soon as the bell tolls?' Alfie felt foolish that he didn't know already.

'If you carry your cloak with you, you'll be able to change into it.'

'I couldn't carry this around all day, though.' Alfie found it hard to hold the weight in a bag.

'No.' She smiled again. 'You decide what article of clothing you want it to be. A jacket, for example and wear it so you have it with you.'

'Wow!' Alfie was taken aback at the brilliance of it. 'But what will happen if I can't decide?' He didn't want to admit that he couldn't do any magic yet.

'During the day it will automatically become a handkerchief, so you can pop it in your pocket,' she said quietly, as if she was letting him into a great secret. 'You don't have to wear it.'

'Thank you.' Alfie smiled at her.

'Why don't you wear it now? It's after six. It would be all right,' urged Derek.

'I know, but I feel guilty because yours is locked in the trunk. Have you remembered the charm you put on the lock?'

Alfie could see that Derek felt like an idiot as he said, 'No! Maybe I'll have to buy another cloak but they're not cheap. Mum will go mad if she thinks I've lost mine.'

'I have enough money left. It was me who shut the trunk.'

'Really? Are you sure?' Derek seemed pleased that he wouldn't have to tell Mrs Bodley, 'I have some money at home, not quite enough but I'll give it to you.'

'That's fine,' said Alfie.

'What colour would you like?' asked the assistant.

'It had better be the same as my old one, which was blue.'

'I'll see if we have one.' She went toward the back of the shop.

Alfie started to imagine himself wearing his cloak.

The assistant came back carrying two cloaks. They were both blue but a slightly different shade.

Derek looked at them. 'That's the same colour as my old one,' he pointed at it, 'but I really like that one.'

Alfie couldn't see a lot of difference between the two. 'I don't think your Mum will notice.'

Derek screwed up his face and twisted it around while he thought about what to do.

'I'll try that one on,' he almost shouted and pointed to the second one, trying to hurry the assistant before he lost his nerve.

She helped him swing it around his shoulders. 'Very smart,' she said calmly.

Derek looked in the mirror and then turned to Alfie. 'Are you sure Mum won't notice?' he whispered, as if Mrs Bodley would hear.

'Fairly sure. And it is a nicer colour.' Alfie felt the weight of the bag he was carrying and wanted to look inside.

Derek made a decision. 'I'll take it!'

'Good. Would you like me to wrap it as well?' asked the assistant.

Derek looked at Alfie.

'Let's wear them!' said Alfie. He couldn't wait any longer.

Derek nodded and Alfie paid the assistant.

Alfie walked along the street and watched his feet come into sight and disappear again under the cloak. He saw his reflection in a shop window and stopped to look properly. He hardly had to move at all to make the colours change. The cloak seemed alive and reminded him of a chameleon.

'Come on. Stop admiring yourself,' said Derek.

'I'm not, I'm admiring my cloak.' Alfie turned towards Derek and followed his gaze to a man walking towards them. He looked very pale and sad.

Derek whispered, 'That's Richard.' He nodded as the man

walked past and greeted them. 'I was sorry to hear about your dog,' said Derek. The man smiled his thanks as he walked away.

'Glad to see that he's alright.' Derek nudged Alfie with his elbow. 'Come on, Wizard Alfie. Let's show the city how good we look.'

Alfie felt like a wizard even though he'd never intentionally done anything magic. Being able to stay in the city at night was enough to prove to him that one day, hopefully soon, he'd perform his first spell.

He was busy imagining it as he walked along. He nodded as Damian walked past and shook his head when he didn't get a response.

'Who was that?' asked Derek, turning up his nose. 'Seems a bit rude.'

'Someone Nigel knows, he's called Damian and also has a potion shop. And a horrible son called Odii,' said Alfie, walking backwards so that he could watch Damian disappear.

'I thought he looked familiar,' said Derek.

'Nigel said Odii and his mother are away.'

'That would explain why we haven't had to deal with him this year. He's horrible.'

'It's good that he's gone to his grandmother's then. Nigel said she's ill, he doesn't think Odii will be back for a while.'

'The longer without him the better! He's friends with Stoop. They stole Bun and Chris's broomsticks once when we were playing at the park, so that they didn't have to walk home. We had to go into the Northeast Quarter to get them back after dark and we were only young!'

Alfie was about to ask what was wrong with the Northeast Quarter when Derek said, 'Look, we're near Nigel's shop.'

'Let's go in and show him our cloaks.'

They went past the shop and through the garden to Nigel's workshop and stood at the door.

'Hello! Nigel!' Alfie called out and was disappointed that Nigel wasn't there. He stepped in and gasped. The whole place had been turned upside down. Everything had been scattered around as if a hurricane had blown through.

Alfie spun around as Nigel silently crept into the room.

'Oh, it's you. I wondered if the burglar had come back,' whispered Nigel.

'What on earth has happened?' Alfie looked around. Derek looked stunned.

'We've only just arrived back. Someone broke in while Mary and I were with your parents, Derek. Upstairs is a mess. They've also gone through everything down here, except the potions.'

Alfie looked around to see what Nigel meant and noticed that all the blue bottles of ingredients and potion vials were still perfectly arranged, not disturbed at all.

'Every drawer has been turned out. The paperwork is scattered everywhere, I can't think what they were after. There doesn't seem to be a pattern to where they looked.' Nigel's cheeks were burning red.

'Can we help?' asked Alfie.

'I don't think so. It's a matter of putting everything back in its correct place. Nothing seems to be missing. We'll just potter along and tidy up. Hopefully it won't take too long.'

'That's good. I'd still like to come and help you on Saturday and deliver potions afterwards.' Alfie hoped he'd still be needed.

'That would be very useful.' Nigel managed a strained smile. He sighed as he looked around at the amount of work he had to do.

As they left Alfie felt angry. 'That's a horrible thing to do to someone.' He couldn't get rid of the niggle that kept popping up. 'I bet it was Damian.'

'Why's that?' asked Derek.

'Well, he was close by just before the burglary.'

'He was, wasn't he? That would have been when Nigel and Mary were out.'

'And he was riffling through Nigel's paperwork the other day. I bet he was trying to get some of Nigel's recipes.'

'That makes sense. They are a lot better than his,' said Derek.

They made their way back to the B&B. The joy of having new cloaks was gone.

CHAPTER NINE

The Northeast Quarter

LATER that week, as Alfie finished supper, he looked around the table. Derek's family had made him feel so welcome. It was fun having so many people around but he missed his father. He half-wished that he could tell him everything, but he kept his letters to him about school, Derek and Ernie the dog. He knew that his father wouldn't believe what happened in Wyckerton each night.

As Alfie changed for bed, he could feel butterflies in his stomach. They seemed to be playing rugby, rather than gently fluttering.

'I don't know what's wrong with me. I feel as if I have an exam tomorrow.' He looked over at Derek.

Derek grinned. 'Don't you remember what's happening?'

Alfie was puzzled. His brows drew together. 'No. Everything's been such a whirl, I don't know what day of the week it is.'

'Tomorrow is Saturday. Nigel is going to give you your first lesson.'

Alfie took a deep breath. *So that's what it is. Good old Derek, reliable as ever.* Alfie didn't know what would happen if Derek wasn't around to tie up all the loose ends.

As he lay in bed, he worried that he'd be useless at magic. He half-hoped that Nigel would still be tidying his workshop so there wouldn't be time for his lesson. At least he'd learn a little bit about potion making. He was still awake an hour later. His rugby-playing butterflies had become sumo wrestlers.

When Alfie woke the next morning, he felt groggy. Tired from staying awake for ages he turned over and snuggled down into his covers to go back to sleep, hoping that he could miss school. Then he remembered it was Saturday! He threw the covers off and jumped up. He ran toward the bathroom and had to hurdle over Fizz as she played on the landing.

'Sorry!' he shouted as he closed the bathroom door, unsure if she'd even seen him.

When he came out, Fizz was waiting patiently.

'Why are you in a hurry. It's not school today?' she said.

Alfie looked at her, amazed that she would hurry to school.

'I'm going to help Nigel in his shop.'

'Oh…' She sounded like it made sense.

He dressed, putting his cloak-handkerchief in his pocket. He ran down the curving stone staircase and then slid down the wide banister rails of the other two.

In the kitchen Mr Bodley and Aunt Edith sat at the table with some guests.

Mrs Bodley was in charge of several pans full of sizzling bacon, eggs and tomatoes. 'Good morning, Alfie. You seem eager?' she said.

'I'm helping Nigel today.' Alfie beamed a smile at her.

'Do you know what you'll be doing?' she asked as she placed a hot breakfast in front of him.

Alfie couldn't help taking a mouthful before he answered. 'I'm supposed to be helping him to make potions and delivering them later. I might just be tidying the workshop today after the burglary.'

'I heard about that. Who would do such a thing?' said Mrs Bodley. Her cheeks turned pink. 'Villains, that's what they are!'

'It wasn't only the shop. They went through their home upstairs as well,' said Mr Bodley.

Alfie wondered whether to mention his thoughts about Damian but decided against it.

Mrs Bodley looked thoughtful. 'I still don't think Nigel knows what they were searching for.'

'Let's hope it's not the beginning of burglaries. We don't usually have trouble in this part of town,' said Mr Bodley.

'Not like the Northeast Quarter,' said Mrs Bodley.

'We all know that trouble starts there.' Aunt Edith perked up. 'If Mervyn had any family, that's where they would live.'

Mrs Bodley looked at her. 'But he doesn't!' she said. 'That's all ended now.'

Alfie looked up, alerted by the sharpness in her voice.

'Let's hope you're right,' said Aunt Edith.

A dark mood had descended over them. Alfie finished his breakfast. He thanked Mrs Bodley as he put his empty plate in the sink. He petted Ernie and left the B&B. As he walked he peered in the shop windows. They were all normal shops again. He watched as some tourists hesitated at a narrow alleyway. They seemed to be checking that it wasn't private before they disappeared along it. Alfie smiled to himself. They clearly thought they were discovering the secrets of Wyckerton as they strolled along the quieter lanes. Little did they really know.

He walked around to the back of Nigel's shop and was surprised that everything inside was tidy.

'Gosh. You must have worked every hour you were awake.'

'We did. We're both pretty exhausted. Though that's more to do with being burgled than tidying up.' Nigel sounded worse than he looked. 'Anyway, if you could help me out in the workshop today, I can finish making up any potions that need to be delivered later. Hopefully I can give your first magic lesson.' His eyes twinkled as he smiled.

Alfie shivered as a tingle ran through his body. He felt very nervous. Hopefully he'd be able to do a little magic by the end of the day.

'I'd also like you to learn about the shop. If you pop through the connecting door and talk to Mary when she has a quiet patch, she can show you the ropes and explain the things that she sells.'

'Hope it's not difficult?' Alfie hardly ever went into shops. The only item he'd ever bought was his cloak.

'No, not difficult but you have to remember that the customers will be non-magics during the day.' Nigel raised his eyebrows.

Of course! 'Why don't they smell the potions being made?' asked Alfie. Then his eyes grew wide. 'Won't they hear us doing magic?'

'The doorway has a senses hex on it. None of their senses will pick anything up.'

'Wow. What happens if they come through the door?'

'How many doors marked *PRIVATE* would you go through?' asked Nigel. 'It would appear locked to non-magics, anyway.'

'Do they have a senses hex at the B&B,' Alfie wondered. 'No one ever comes in to ask if there are rooms available.'

'Yes. It's just another layer of protection in case non-magics don't see that it says *No Vacancies*. The hex also covers the windows. Passers-by can't see in.'

'Wow!' said Alfie again. That was why everything continued to be magical inside the B&B during the day. He remembered talking to the guests about hexes. 'Nigel, one of the guests said he has a senses hex on his house but he lives among non-magics. Would it still work?'

'Definitely. A wizard's home is his castle. It needs to be a haven.'

It was busier than Alfie expected a health food shop would be. Non-magics kept entering, looking at the wide selection of quality food. It was loose in large wooden buckets. Scoops rested on top. For a while he was whizzing back and forth between the shop and the workshop but by three o'clock, it became quieter. He managed to spend more time with Nigel.

At first, the smell of the ingredients was revolting. As Nigel explained what he was mixing, Alfie became so involved he didn't notice the heavy, spicy smell anymore. He watched as each item was added to the cauldron. Such tiny amounts sometimes that Alfie was surprised that they found their way into the pot. Nigel weighed small quantities on a delicate set of scales. The tiny weights could have been buttons. The two weighing pans were so shiny every speck slid off. A bigger set of scales weighed larger amounts. Nigel either rubbed his thumb and forefinger together to break the surface of the kernels and seeds or he used a pestle and mortar to crush them. Some potions took time to make. They used fewer ingredients but had to be heated carefully in the cauldron for an exact amount of time. Others didn't need heating and were put into the bottle and shaken. Alfie doubted that they would work as well. It seemed as if they were made with less care.

When Mary was busy in the shop, Alfie helped her to serve customers. The long wooden counter had an old till at one end. Paper bags of various sizes were laid out in small piles ready to use. The scales were enormous compared with Nigel's two sets. A stack of copper weights stood by the base. He couldn't believe how many non-magics came in. Sometimes they had to queue but Mary managed to keep them all happy.

Alfie watched as a lady chose a face-cream that was on display. 'Everyone has commented on how youthful I look. I've only been using it for a month,' she said.

'That will be the natural ingredients energising your skin.' Mary smiled. 'I use it and I'm ninety-four.'

'You're not a day over fifty-five!' exclaimed the lady and left the shop, still grinning.

Alfie took a sneaky look at Mary. He didn't know her actual age but she didn't look ninety-four.

The shop became quiet. 'You run along back to Nigel. I'm fine topping up the buckets,' said Mary.

Alfie nodded and went through the connecting door.

Nigel had whizzed through his potion making, which left some free time.

'How shall we begin your lesson?' asked Nigel.

Alfie raised his shoulders, only able to whisper, 'You're the teacher.'

'Oh oh,' Nigel looked at him, 'what have I let myself in for?' Alfie watched as Nigel thought, then he took a deep breath and looked directly at him. 'First, Alfie, magic starts from within. Most people possess a confidence that it *will* happen,' he said. 'Probably the most important thing to remember is that you mustn't try too hard to *force* something to happen.'

Alfie smiled nervously. A short time ago he hadn't even known that magic existed. Now Nigel was telling him not to try too hard when performing it! He wanted to giggle.

'Whatever spell you're performing, your balance is essential. The way you stand helps.'

Nigel stood opposite Alfie with his feet apart, his right foot slightly ahead of his left. He bounced on his bent knees.

Alfie mimicked him.

'Good. Now, if you feel really stable, you can stand without your knees bent, but keep them relaxed.'

Alfie straightened his knees and nodded. He felt odd, finding it hard to believe that he'd be able to do magic but scared that he might not. He didn't believe Derek that he'd performed some already and had mended that cat-flap.

'How you move your hands depends on what spell you're casting.' Nigel performed some different hand movements to give Alfie an idea of what he meant. 'I think we'll start with the movement spell.' He placed a pencil on the bench top. 'Try and make it move,' he instructed.

'How? I mean, should it roll or jump or stand on its end?' asked Alfie.

'Any of those would be good,' encouraged Nigel as he gave Alfie a sideways glance and smiled. 'As you move your arm, say *Momentum* so that it fits in with the movement.'

Nigel moved his arm decisively as he spoke the word. The pencil rolled along about twelve inches. He picked it up and returned it to its original position. He looked at Alfie reassuringly.

Alfie took a deep breath. He found it hard to stand correctly, relax his knees, move his hands and talk at the right time. He remembered Derek doing magic. He tried to swoosh his hand at the pencil. Nothing happened. His fingers folded into a loose fist as his concentration made him forget his surroundings.

Nigel quietly said, 'Relax. Don't think of it as being *under* your control. See it roll along in your mind's eye as if it's already happening.' He put his hand on Alfie's tense shoulder. 'Relax,' he said again.

Alfie looked at him. The movement hurt his neck. 'Ouch.' He stopped moving, hoping the pain would end. He wasn't sure how long he had been staring at the pencil but his body had become rigid. He rolled his shoulders in a circular motion and began to loosen up.

He turned back to the pencil. He straightened his arm, said *'Momentum!'* and flicked his hand at the same time.

When the pencil rolled a quarter of a turn towards him, he whooped with pleasure.

Nigel clapped. 'Well done! That was stunning for your first attempt.' Nigel seemed to be as pleased as Alfie.

He practised for a little longer until they needed to make more potions.

The day became even better when the city chimes rang out. Alfie quickly removed the handkerchief from his pocket and gripped it tightly as it grew heavier and changed into his beloved cloak. He swung it around his shoulders and glanced at Nigel. He had changed into his cloak. Alfie felt as though he truly belonged.

Alfie looked through the connecting door to the shop and watched as pots, mini-cauldrons and potions replaced the food and provisions. The mood of the shop changed too. It felt calmer but more serious.

Mary spotted him. 'I'm going upstairs to start supper now. Can you ask Nigel to watch the shop?'

Alfie grinned. 'He said his stomach was rumbling.'

'Then he'll be pleased to know I'm making potted partridge with my special ingredient.'

When Alfie told Nigel he looked pleased. 'My favourite.'

'What's in it?' asked Alfie.

'She won't tell me but I know she has an essential oil and herb mixture that she makes herself. She won't even let me collect the ingredients from the suppliers.'

Alfie wished he could taste it.

Alfie and Nigel manned the shop. Alfie was still grinning at the thought of the pencil moving. His face ached by the time he'd served a few customers. It didn't matter how much it hurt, he couldn't stop smiling.

Now that the shop had changed from Nurture by Nature to Powerful Potions, the customers were all magic. They wanted all sorts of mixtures: weed-killer for bindweed, crop fertilisers and painkillers. A lady wanted a tonic to keep her cat healthy as she looked after her kittens. A man wanted an inside-outside potion for his dog.

As the man left, Alfie couldn't resist asking, 'What's that for?'

'It allows his dog to be normal outside but when the dog goes into his small house, it doesn't smell or moult. Much less trouble.'

'Wow, so he can buy the size dog he really wants!'

'Guess so.' Nigel laughed.

The bell on the shop door jangled as it opened. Alfie looked up to see Richard standing at the entrance. He was pale and unwell. His eyes were sunken and surrounded by dark, tired skin.

'Hello Richard, it's good to see you again. How can I help?' Nigel seemed pleased to see him.

'Can you make me a potion to reduce my pain? I seem to hurt all over at the moment.' Richard tried to return his friend's smile. He would have been a handsome man when he was younger. Alfie wondered if pain alone could change a face.

'Take a seat. I'll be a few minutes. Nothing serious, I hope?' asked Nigel, before he disappeared out the back.

'I don't think so. Probably just missing my dog.' Sadness passed across Richard's face as he sat down.

Alfie found the courage to talk. 'It must be awful when your dog dies. I love playing with Ernie.'

'It was,' said Richard. 'Is Ernie your dog?'

'Yes,' said Alfie, then corrected himself. 'No, he's the Bodley's but I live with them at the B&B and help to look after him.'

Richard nodded and then looked at the floor as he waited, making it obvious that he didn't want to talk.

'Here you go.' Nigel came back into the shop holding a full vial. 'Take three drops. You will feel better within minutes.'

'Do you mind if I take some now. Then I'll be feeling better by the time I get home.'

'That's a good idea, I'll get you a dropper.' Nigel started to leave the room again.

'I'll go.' Alfie nipped out of the door. When he returned, they were laughing together. He could see what good friends they were.

Richard swallowed some medicine. 'It was good to catch up, old friend,' he said to Nigel as he left.

When Richard had gone, Nigel explained that they had been best friends as boys. 'His father worked at the law firm. When I'd finished helping my father, we'd meet and go to the park.' He chuckled at the memory. 'We'd get up to all sorts of mischief, including Manhunt!'

Manhunt! That's the game of chase that had nearly hit Aunt Edith. He recalled the broom riders swooping across the city trying to catch each other.

Nigel continued, 'Richard has always been an extremely powerful sorcerer, very capable. He always learnt things much quicker than I ever could.' Nigel stood for a moment longer and then said, 'It all changes when you get married and have to work full time, though. Not that I'd want it any different. I'm very happy with my life with Mary.'

They left the shop and went into the back to tidy up and get the deliveries ready. Nigel placed the full potion vials in a special bag with little sleeves to stop them clinking together. Alfie started to put the blue bottles of ingredients back on the shelves. As they were all numbered, it was an easy job.

'Is the blue significant?' asked Alfie as he admired them.

'Not really, it's more of a trademark.'

'I like the colour.' Alfie smiled. He picked up another bottle. It wasn't smooth like the rest. 'Why do some of the bottles have grooves?'

'Because they hold poisons. I can feel which bottle I'm holding, even in the dark.'

Alfie put the bottle on the shelf, uneasy that some ingredients were dangerous.

'That seems to be everything. You can start the deliveries now,' said Nigel, placing a list of customers and a map by the bag. He paused and turned to Alfie. 'Maybe I ought to come with you. Some of the deliveries are in the Northeast Quarter this week. It's not the safest part of the city.'

Alfie's mouth turned down at the edges. 'Don't worry, I'm sure Ernie will look after me. You need to watch the shop while Mary's making your supper.'

'That's true. The customers will be pleased with earlier deliveries today. I usually do them after supper,' said Nigel. 'Make sure you do the ones in the Northeast Quarter first ... before it gets dark.'

'Okay. Thanks for a brilliant day and teaching me to move the pencil.' Alfie was chuffed.

'You're a good student. Keep practising. I'll see you next Saturday.'

Alfie picked up the heavy bag, the list and the map. He headed back to the B&B to get Ernie before he started the delivery route.

With the heavy bag on his shoulder, he decided to start with the closest houses. Ernie trotted along beside him as Alfie knocked on doors to leave the potions. The customers were pleased to see him. They took the bottles and chatted. Alfie felt very capable as he marched along in his cloak, watching the buildings glow in the evening sun.

When he had delivered half of his load, he left the main street again to find an address. He passed a dilapidated old house being held up by supportive scaffolding. It had the same black timber frame as the B&B. The joints at the ends of the timbers had split, leaving great gaps. The plaster between the timbers was cracked. Chunks of plaster had already fallen out. The deep crevices that were left seemed to be filled with dust, held together by horsehair. Alfie moved closer and noticed that some of the window frames were turning to sawdust. The open windows were hanging dangerously. It seemed that a gentle gust of wind would knock down the whole building. Alfie stood against the railing that was being used to cordon it off. As he moved back, another chunk of plaster fell, breaking into lumps and dust as it hit the ground. A sign

attached to the barrier warned people to keep out. The building
was only fit for demolition.

After the delivery further up the road Alfie re-joined the main
street without going past the derelict house again. As he made his
way to the area for the final deliveries, he was relieved that the bag
was lighter. The wide sunny streets of the main parts of the city
were replaced with narrower cobbled alleyways. Alfie stopped to
look at the map to make sure he was going in the right direction.
He checked street names and realised that he was heading towards
the Northeast Quarter. This was where Nigel had told him to start
the deliveries. It was dusk and he felt cross with himself for
forgetting. *This place is horrible.* He tugged Ernie closer, glad that he'd
brought him along. He looked around for the various addresses.
His skin prickled as he went past a few people. Almost everyone
looked nasty. They were dressed in black cloaks and watched slyly
from half-closed eyes. Alfie didn't dare make eye contact. They'd
probably see it as a direct challenge.

He had never been anywhere so gloomy. It felt as if his
happiness was being sucked away. He wanted to shrink, unwilling
to touch the dark buildings. He was sure that they were leaning
towards him, trying to absorb him into their shadowy walls. Anyone
that lived here must have something dark to hide.

If he had started his deliveries here, he would be back in the
safer parts of the city by now. Next week he would listen to Nigel
and plan his route properly. *Last one,* he thought, relieved as he
removed the last bottle from the bag.

Alfie shuffled backwards into the recess that housed the door,
keeping an eye on anyone who passed. He glanced down at the dirty
floor tiles. The greasy dust was so thick it had started to creep up
the walls. He banged on the door. The doorknob twisted. Two
hands in fingerless gloves curled around the door and pulled. A
face appeared, followed by a body as the stiff door opened.

The man smiled, his teeth long and yellow. 'Good evening, how
can I help you?' His voice was polite but he exuded menace. A
shiver ran down Alfie's spine.

'I have a delivery from the potion shop.' Alfie held it out. He hoped this was the right person. He didn't want to hang around longer than necessary.

The man nodded. He reached out, shaking slightly. His knuckles turned white as his hand closed around the vial. He attempted to breathe in deeply but his eyes closed with the effort.

Alfie stood still, determined not to show that he was scared.

'I'll get you some money.' The man wheezed. Alfie watched him walk away. The house was very dark inside, making all the furnishings look grimy.

The coins Alfie was given in payment felt cold in his hand, as if the house they had come from had never known warmth. He stepped back into the lane. As he took the first footsteps towards home, he looked up into the faces of passers-by. The coins that he was holding suddenly felt large. He worried that they were aware of them. He slipped them into his pocket, relieved as they fell from his hand.

The narrow lanes were frightening but as he turned a corner, his stride faltered. He couldn't decide if the totally empty street ahead of him was worse than the previous lanes with their gloomy figures. The light was fading. The air had become damp as the night descended. As he passed a dark alleyway something grabbed his attention. A concealed figure relentlessly walked round in circles. Alfie turned to leave quickly but he overheard mumblings that made him pause.

'So what. So what. It can't be helped. Nigel will die when I've completed my part… I have to have it … It can't have been destroyed. Only he can do it but he's too sentimental … It's far more significant than he thinks … He promised me. He can't go back on it…'

Alfie slammed his hand over his mouth to muffle his gasp. *Not Nigel!* He could only see a dark shape but he could feel the desperation oozing from it. He turned and ran out of the Northeast Quarter as quickly as his legs would go. Ernie ran along beside him with his tail tucked between his hind legs, aware of Alfie's fear.

The streets started to become wider and well lit. Alfie stopped and rested against a building to catch his breath. People looked at him oddly as they passed. He managed to calm himself and wondered what to do. *Derek will know.*

He pushed himself away from the wall and walked back towards the B&B. His mind was replaying what he had heard when he felt a plop on his shoulder. He hardly had to look to know that a pigeon had messed on his cloak.

'Eeew.' He saw the squidgy white and green lump. 'Yuck!'

It started to seep into the weave of the material. It would be impossible to get it all out by the time he arrived back at the B&B. He looked around for something to wipe it off. He needed a stick, but couldn't see one. *Why is it on my cloak and not my school uniform?* He picked up a small twig and tried to scrape it off but it snapped in half, almost pushing his thumb into the mess.

'Dregs!' Annoyed, he moved his hand in a sweeping movement over the mess and said, *'Momentum!'*

His jaw dropped as every trace of poo left his cloak and hit the pavement. He moved his face closer. The material was spotless. It wasn't even damp. He laughed aloud as he looked around.

Ernie sat patiently. Alfie grabbed his lead and ran the rest of the way back to the B&B, his success only spoiled by what he had heard earlier in the Northeast Quarter.

CHAPTER TEN

Mr Locksley

DEREK was sitting in the snug off the side of the sitting room when Alfie eventually found him.

'Oh, Alfie, you'll have to come and see the market next time it's here. It's never boring. Even brilliant in the day when the non-magics are there.' Derek was so excited Alfie couldn't get a word in. 'And then, when they've all gone, it gets even better -'

'Someone is trying to kill Nigel!' Alfie blurted out.

It stopped Derek immediately. 'What! What do you mean?' he asked.

'I overheard someone while I was delivering potions. They need him to die.'

Derek looked stunned. 'Did you see who it was?'

Almost to himself, Alfie said, 'He was a shadow. He needed something to help do it. It didn't sound like he was going to attack Nigel directly.' He chewed his cheek, thinking. 'Damian was looking for something at Nigel's when he was shuffling that paperwork about.' He looked at Derek.

'So?'

'I think the shadowy figure was Damian. Maybe he wasn't interested in Nigel's recipes for potions, after all. Maybe he was looking for the object to kill Nigel. He must have thought it was at Nigel's. Clearly he didn't find it or he wouldn't still be looking.'

'I can see Damian being behind it. He probably hates Nigel because he is so much better at potion making than him,' said Derek.

Alfie nodded. 'Do you think your parents can help?'

'No! Mum won't like us snooping. Specially as we haven't any proof.'

'Okay. I guess that we're going to have to find this object first.' Alfie's mysteries didn't usually include magic. 'I'll see if I can find anything in a book.' He headed for the study. One wall was covered in bookshelves. Books for everyone: modern novels, biographies and children's stories from fairy-tales to young adult books. Towards the top shelves the binding of the books looked older. Alfie scanned the titles. They were more like what he'd expected to see in a magic house: *How To Make The Perfect Potion*, *Possessing Magic*, and *Mastering Magic*. Alfie reached up and tried to pull a book off the shelf. His finger hooked into the leather spine of an old book. He could feel the weight before he'd even lifted it. He knew that he'd drop it if he didn't get hold of the end properly.

He grabbed a chair and started to drag it toward the shelves. The back legs bounced across the carpet. He straightened it and raised his foot to step on the expensive cloth that covered the seat. The chair slid out of the way so that his foot hit the floor with a thump.

'Hey, what the heck…' Alfie stood up straight.

The chair had split itself across the middle horizontally and the back support tipped over the seat. When it had finished, it had become a set of steps.

'Gosh…' Alfie grinned as he climbed up to get the book he wanted. It was unbelievably heavy, bigger than any book he'd ever read. It would be easier to ask people if they knew a way of putting a death curse on Nigel. *I don't know what's possible in the magic world*, he thought.

He carried it to the desk and plonked it down. He opened it and looked at the index. The language was really old and hard to understand. Some words had an *e* on the end or an *f* in the place of *s*. Reading about magic wasn't going to be easy. Maybe it would be better to put it back and find something else. He decided against it. He took down a few more books and made a small pile. *I'll get Derek to help me look through them.* As he walked towards the door, the set of steps changed back into a chair.

Alfie was in a world of his own as he came out of the study and bumped into a solid, squidgy being.

'Sorry,' he said, and stepped backwards to get out of the way.

'Don't worry about it.' The body's voice was rasping and breathless.

Alfie tried to focus. The man was so large that he even made Chris look tiny. He was so beefy that to see all of him, Alfie would have had to be at the other end of the hallway.

Mrs Bodley appeared from behind him, Alfie hadn't realised that she was there. 'Alfie, this is Mr Locksley. He'll be staying at the B&B for a while.'

'Pleased to meet you, sir,' said Alfie politely. He reached out his hand but withdrew it quickly, scared to get too close in case the man fell over and squashed him.

Mr Locksley tried to smile but his skin was so stretched it refused to change shape. Alfie backed into the study so that they could continue past. He giggled as he overheard the conversation Mrs Bodley and Mr Locksley had as they walked toward the sitting room.

'We'll be having supper very shortly. Would you like a cup of tea and a biscuit while you wait?' asked Mrs Bodley.

'A cup of tea sounds wonderful if it's not too much trouble. Don't bring biscuits though. I'll wait for supper. I don't like to eat between meals,' said Mr Locksley.

'This way then.' Mrs Bodley stopped at the sitting room door and ushered him in. 'Make yourself comfortable. I'll fetch the tea.' Alfie knew she would bring biscuits as well.

Derek came into view as Alfie was leaving the study for the second time.

'Did you see that man? I thought I'd be stuck in the snug forever. He nearly takes up the whole sitting room,' said Derek, still looking over his shoulder.

Alfie laughed. 'Come and see these books,' he said and went back into the study.

Derek flicked through them and made a decision. 'It's going to take ages to read these. Let's take them up to our room so that we can spread them out.'

They each carried half of the pile. As they left the study, Mr Bodley came through the front door.

'Ah, good,' he said, and popped a bag of sweets on top of the books. 'I've eaten enough of those. You two can finish them.'

'Thanks,' said Derek, as if it happened regularly.

'Just don't tell your Mum they came from me.' Mr Bodley winked at them.

They managed to climb the three sets of stairs.

'I'll just check that Ernie has water. We did a lot of running to get back here,' said Alfie, wishing he'd thought of it before.

He walked into the sitting room. Ernie was sitting patiently by Mr Locksley's armchair. As Alfie moved closer he noticed that the biscuits Mrs Bodley had brought were still on a small table with a half-drunk cup of tea. Alfie felt guilty. *Maybe you don't eat a lot.* The armchair strained under Mr Locksley's weight. He was holding a necklace with blue stones and an unusual clasp. He put it down on the side table and picked something up from his lap. Ernie's head rocked from side to side as if he didn't understand what was happening.

Alfie crept up so that he could watch Ernie. As he edged closer, he noticed that Mr Locksley was knitting. Then he saw what was being knitted! The needles were whizzing twenty to the dozen. When complete, the most scrumptious cakes were freeing themselves from the needles. Mr Locksley stopped when his lap was full.

'At last, it works perfectly. I'm sure everyone will love these!' He looked around to make sure he was alone.

Alfie dived out of sight.

'Better hide the evidence,' said Mr Locksley, letting out a gruff laugh before he stuffed all the cakes into his mouth. He started knitting again as he chewed.

Alfie crept out of the room without disturbing either Ernie or Mr Locksley.

CHAPTER ELEVEN

Edward

ALFIE walked into the almost empty classroom alone. Derek was running an errand for Mr Kalm. Alfie nodded at Martha and Jazz but they were looking elsewhere. When he saw who they were looking at, he wanted to turn around and leave the room.

Edward was leaning over a desk. 'So, I'm going to need yours,' he said to the boy sitting down.

John was standing close by, smirking.

'But I haven't done my homework, either,' said the boy.

'Let's have a look, shall we?' Edward grabbed his bag and pulled out some sheets of paper. 'Hmm, this looks like it will do,' he said as he punched the boy in the arm. 'That's for lying to me.'

'Nice one,' said John.

Alfie took a step towards them. 'Give it back, Edward,' he said.

Edward looked across the room. 'What are you going to do about it, Walters?'

Alfie breathed in. 'Nothing,' he said as he sat down at a desk wishing he could use magic.

Edward rubbed off the boy's name and wrote his own. Other pupils started to come into the classroom.

Derek sat down beside Alfie as Bun and Chris walked into the room. Alfie hadn't had the chance to talk privately with them yet. He didn't want to discuss what he'd heard about Nigel and his suspicions about Damian by sending notes during lessons. When the homework was collected at the end of the class, no one said anything about what Edward had done earlier.

Alfie checked his timetable. 'Double sports next.'

'Hope it's rugby,' said Chris as they made their way to the changing rooms.

When they had changed into their kit, they went to the playing field and joined a crowd of boys waiting to be told what to do. As Mr Becks, one of the sports teachers, passed him, Alfie puffed up his chest and hoped that Mr Becks wouldn't notice his skinny knees.

'We want to make the selections for the rugby teams today. Can I have anyone taller than this boy,' Mr Becks put his hand on the top of a boy's head, 'over on that side with Mr James.' He indicated where he wanted them to go. Chris and Bun moved away. Alfie was pleased to see that Derek stayed in his group.

'Where shall I go, Sir?' asked a boy who made Chris look normal.

'Very funny, Eric,' said Mr Becks, 'now scoot, before I make you help me teach instead of playing!'

Eric laughed and moved over to the group of larger boys.

Mr Becks kept the group of shorter boys. They warmed up with stretches before they ran around the field twice.

Then they had to choose a partner and run while passing the ball back and forth.

Alfie and Derek started passing normally but it soon became more enthusiastic. Derek threw the ball to Alfie. It headed straight for his face before he caught it.

'Oops, sorry!' said Derek innocently, fighting a smile. 'My hand slipped.'

Alfie looked at him and knew that it wasn't an accident.

'Don't worry, we can't all be perfect!' Alfie launched the ball so hard it slipped through Derek's fingers and he had to run to fetch it. 'Looks like I'm not that good either!' he said, chuckling.

Mr Becks mixed the two original groups and organised a quick match to see them all in action. Alfie, Derek and Bun were on the same team. *I suppose that's fair, Chris could take on all three of us at once.*

Alfie enjoyed the speed of the game. Passes between him and Derek were spot-on now they were on the same team. Alfie felt energised as he dived, doing tackles. His lungs hurt as he ran full pelt down the pitch. His face smacked into the mud as he was tackled. When he stood up, he hadn't run as far as he thought he had but he still grinned. A combined tackle with Derek wasn't enough to bring Chris to the ground as he charged the length of the pitch to score a try. Alfie was pleased when Eric did the same as Chris to even the score.

At the end of the session Mr Becks spoke to all of them. 'Well done, I think you all tried hard.' He looked impressed and went on to congratulate those who had made the team. Alfie was disappointed that he and Derek weren't included.

As the four of them walked back to the changing rooms, Alfie looked at Bun and said, 'I didn't see if you and Chris made the team.'

'Yeah, we both did,' said Bun. 'Eric made captain.'

'Well done.'

'You could have made captain, Chris,' said Derek.

'Nah. Wouldn't want to. I'd have to plan stuff. I'd rather just grab the ball and run as the opposition scatters!'

'I suppose it does suit Eric,' said Derek. 'He'll make a good captain. He loves rugby. I bet he'll come up with some good tactics, too.'

Alfie took longer to change than the others. By the time they were ready he was still only half-dressed.

Chris fidgeted. 'I'm starving. Do you mind if we go to lunch? We'll get yours. See you at the table,' he said.

'Okay. Will they let you take an extra tray?'

'We'll let Bun deal with that,' said Derek as they left.

Alfie shoved his clothes in his kit bag as the door to the changing room opened. Two boys came in and Alfie felt uneasy when he saw through the racks of hanging clothes that one of them was Edward. He guessed that the other was John.

'Did you hear that boy. I love it when they stutter. He promised me his lunch money for a week if I didn't spill ink all over his homework,' said Edward.

'And you told him a week wasn't enough. Classic,' responded John.

Alfie would have recognised their spiteful voices even if he hadn't seen them. He held his breath. He had never been able to cope with Edward. He sighed with relief as they left. He sat down on the bench and waited a few minutes before he left the changing room. He didn't want to face them again.

He made his way towards the canteen, walking behind Martha and Jazz as they watched Edward shove a smaller boy out of his way. Alfie looked at the ground, hating himself for being so cowardly.

'You took ages,' said Derek, when Alfie arrived at the table.

'Mm,' said Alfie, not wanting to say why. He ate slowly even though the others had nearly finished their lunch.

When they had cleared their lunch trays, they made their way to the far side of the sports field. As they walked, Alfie explained to Bun and Chris what he'd heard in the Northeast Quarter and his suspicions of Damian.

'So you think the figure was Damian?' asked Bun.

'Sounds like it was to me,' said Chris, convinced.

Alfie nodded. 'We need to discover what the object is and find it first,' he said.

'It sounds like you've done this sort of thing before,' said Chris.

'This is what he's like when he thinks he's found a mystery,' said Derek, who had been through it many times before.

'We'll follow your lead.' Chris was impressed.

'I agree.' Bun couldn't hide his excitement. He appeared to love a challenge, too.

'We still need to check everything. Your fathers have known Nigel for years. Can you ask them if he has any enemies.' Alfie looked at them to check that they agreed. 'Be careful though. We don't want to alert Damian.'

Bun and Chris fidgeted as if they couldn't wait to find out about Damian.

'I'll drop in at Nigel's shop and ask him as well,' said Alfie.

'You can't just blurt out that someone is trying to kill him.' Derek seemed alarmed.

'Don't worry, I'll be tactful.' Alfie didn't feel too confident.

*

Back at the B&B, Alfie decided to walk Ernie before going to see Nigel. The bell had tolled. He pulled on his cloak before grabbing some biscuits from the tin to get him through to suppertime. He walked along by the river, making his way to the park. Ernie was off his lead, jogging along beside him. Alfie stopped next to a shallow area of water and started skimming stones across the width of the river. Ernie avoided the water as he excitedly ran between its edge and Alfie.

'Go in, scaredy cat!' encouraged Alfie, but there was no way Ernie was going to get his feet wet.

Another dog appeared and ran full speed into the water as its lady owner came and stood beside Alfie.

'My dog can't go past water without getting soaked,' she said. 'Don't encourage your dog too much!'

Alfie watched the dog. 'Do you have to teach them to swim?'

'No. They just go in further each time until they're out of their depth. It's natural.' She called her dog as she continued on her walk.

Alfie felt like that about magic. At the moment he was well out of his depth. Eventually he hoped he'd find that it came naturally.

He turned around and headed back, deciding not to go to the park. He needed to talk to Nigel. It wouldn't help to put it off.

He stood outside Nigel's shop, and gently kicked the edge of the pavement. Derek had been right. He could hardly say, "Oh, by the way, Nigel, someone wants you dead." He shook his head and took another deep breath. *I like mysteries, not discussions. How do I start the conversation?* He walked back and forth, moving towards the path that led to Nigel's workshop for the tenth time and stopped, no closer to a decision than when he'd first arrived. He mumbled to himself, not realising that he wasn't alone.

'Are you going to be out there all evening?' Nigel poked his head out of the shop door.

Alfie panicked that he'd been overheard. 'No, I was just going to come in and talk to you.'

Nigel came out of the shop and walked towards him.

'Let's go into the workshop then.' He started to walk down the side path as if he knew Alfie was worried.

Alfie followed. He watched Nigel's heels peep out from under his cloak as he walked ahead.

'Someone is trying to kill you!' It was out before he'd known he was going to speak. *Idiot!* He wanted to kick himself.

Nigel stopped and turned around, frowning.

'Why on earth would you think that?'

'I overheard someone the other night when I was delivering potions in the Northeast Quarter. Can you think of anyone who would want to harm you?' Alfie didn't want to suggest Damian until Nigel had had time to think.

Nigel shook his head.

'Honestly, Alfie, thank you for caring but I don't have any enemies. I've never hurt anyone in my life.'

'But they said your name…'

'All of it? Surname too?'

'Only Nigel,' Alfie had to admit, 'but I *know* it was you.'

'There must be loads of Nigels around. It's a common name.'

'But…' Alfie faltered. He couldn't explain how he knew that it was this Nigel.

'It's not me. Don't worry,' said Nigel gently.

'I think it was Damian.'

'Why?'

'You're a better potion maker than him.'

'That's no reason to want someone harmed.'

'It wasn't harmed. It was dead.' Alfie tried to make him understand.

'I'm sorry, Alfie, but I think you imagined it all. My death wouldn't benefit Damian. He wouldn't be able to poach my potions. He needs me to explain them to him.' Nigel tried to make a joke of it but became more serious. 'I'm not sure Damian would like things like this being said about him.' He started to walk along the path again.

Alfie looked after him and knew that he wouldn't get anywhere by continuing.

'I'd better get back to the B&B. Ernie needs feeding.'

Nigel stood still. He raised his shoulders and gently shook his head. Alfie turned on his heel and quickly walked away with Ernie.

CHAPTER TWELVE

Broomsticks

ALFIE and Derek lay in their beds and talked about Nigel. Alfie tucked his arms behind his head. He decided he didn't want to think about Nigel's situation anymore. Living in Wyckerton was meant to be fun.

'I'm trying to imagine flying around on a broomstick!'

'You'd love it,' said Derek.

'It has to be amazing,' said Alfie. 'Can you fall off?'

'Not really, unless you crash,' said Derek. 'It's a fairly safe way to get around.'

'Maybe one day I'll have a go,' said Alfie as he rolled over and fell asleep.

The next morning Mrs Bodley was already in the kitchen when Alfie entered. As usual, breakfast was ready. Mr Bodley and Derek were tucking into their food.

'It's Nigel and Mary's anniversary next month. They've been married for twenty-five years,' said Mrs Bodley.

Alfie was amazed that anyone could be married for that long.

'Are they celebrating?' asked Mr Bodley.

Mrs Bodley shook her head. 'I don't think so. Nigel's not really one for parties.'

Derek wolfed down the last of his breakfast and jumped up from the table.

'Hurry up, Alfie, I don't want to be late for school.'

Alfie looked up. 'I've only just started.'

'Don't chew so much then. Just swallow it.'

'Derek, don't be silly,' said Mrs Bodley. 'Tidy your dishes away. You can sit and wait for Alfie.'

Alfie quickly finished his breakfast and they left for school.

'Why are we hurrying?' asked Alfie, finding it hard to keep up.

Derek slowed down slightly.

'No reason,' he said.

'You're not usually this eager to get to school.'

'I just want to talk to Bun and Chris, that's all.' Derek didn't seem to want to tell Alfie why. He assumed it was about Nigel. He didn't push it.

As they arrived at school, Derek nodded at Martha and Jazz who were sitting by the entrance. They were perched on the wall, lazily swinging their legs as they chatted.

'You're here early. What's happening?' asked Derek.

'We went on a mission last night. We're waiting to see the result,' said Jazz.

Alfie couldn't imagine what they had been up to. 'What did you do?' he asked.

'We flew out to Edward's house and let his bike tyres down. He'll have to pump them up or walk to school. I bet he's too lazy to use a pump,' said Martha.

'And he lives miles away,' added Jazz, grinning.

Alfie cringed at the mention of Edward's name.

'Are you always going to punish bullies?' asked Derek.

'Only until they stop harassing smaller kids,' said Jazz.

Alfie looked at Martha. Surely there weren't many children smaller than her.

Derek seemed to have forgotten that he'd been in a hurry. He sat on the wall next to Martha and waited.

Alfie felt a little bit guilty. Maybe he should stand up to Edward. The idea made his stomach turn. He wasn't ready yet.

'Shh, here he is,' whispered Martha. 'Doesn't look like he's got much energy left for bullying today.' She smirked.

'Serves him right,' said Jazz.

Alfie sneakily looked over his shoulder at Edward as he shuffled along the drive toward the school building. He tried not to feel too smug but it was good to see that Edward was miserable.

Bun and Chris were waiting for them in their classroom. Alfie was eager to discuss what they had found out about Nigel but they couldn't until they were in a private place. Alfie and Derek hadn't had any luck but he hoped that Bun and Chris would have some news.

Alfie couldn't contain himself once they were out of earshot at the break. 'Did either of you find out anything?' he asked.

'My Dad and Nigel share a lot of friends. He thought the only person who would benefit from Nigel not being around would be Damian,' said Bun.

'I even asked my uncles. They said Nigel was a caring, clever man. The only person they could think of with a grudge against Nigel was Damian,' said Chris. 'They said he's an awful man who only ever thinks of himself.'

'Just like Odii,' said Derek.

Bun and Chris immediately started moaning.

'Slimy pig! Do you remember when he stole our broomsticks?'

'Yeah. And when he stuck my shoes to the ground because I wouldn't ask Dad to give him a deal on a new broomstick,' said Bun. 'Took ages for the spell to wear off, I was late for supper.'

'Maybe your father should invent a trick broom that would fly him away forever!' said Alfie.

'Would be good, but wouldn't do much for Dad's broom shop's reputation.'

'But he could call it the "Odii Ouster".' Chris laughed at his own joke.

'I'm glad he's away this year,' said Derek.

So was Alfie, he didn't want to have to deal with any more bullies. 'If your fathers both agree, that settles it. It must be Damian, nothing seems to lead to anyone else,' he said, pleased when the others agreed.

Deep in thought as he made his way to the next lesson, Alfie looked back expecting the others to have followed but they weren't there. They eventually came through the door, caught up in conversation.

'Did you think of anything else?' Alfie asked quietly.

They jolted to a stop and seemed worried that he might have overheard. They all looked at him blankly.

'About Nigel...?' prompted Alfie, frowning.

'Oh no, we weren't talking about that,' said Derek.

Alfie waited but none of them spoke.

'Okay...' He walked over to his desk and sat down. The others started to talk again, only sitting down when Mrs Stott came into the room. Mrs Stott snarled at everyone, making the double geography lesson seem even longer. *Why do I need to know about coastal erosion?* Alfie looked forward to lunch as his stomach started to rumble.

They joined the end of the lunch queue, all too hungry to speak. Bun and Chris were given larger portions because they sometimes helped the dinner ladies carry the food deliveries. After eating, they walked to the far side of the sports field. There they chewed over their thoughts about Nigel. As they walked back, Alfie found himself alone again. The others had hung back, deep in conversation.

'What are you discussing?' he asked as they caught up with him.

They pretended they didn't know what he was talking about.

'Tomorrow,' said Chris vaguely.

Bun's head whipped around as he looked at Chris.

'We were just discussing what we'd do tomorrow while you're at Nigel's.' Bun spoke slightly too quickly.

'Yes, that's all.' Derek's voice sounded odd, as well.

Alfie looked at all three of them. There was more to it than what they were going to do on a Saturday. What didn't they want him to know?

The afternoon lessons passed slowly but as they all walked home, they talked and joked as usual. Alfie almost forgot that they had spent some of the day excluding him.

*

As they prepared for bed, Alfie wanted to ask Derek what he had been plotting with Bun and Chris, but decided against it. *They'll tell me when they're ready.*

'I've been thinking about Nigel and Mary's anniversary. He's helped me a lot with my magic. I'd like to do something for them,' said Alfie.

Derek nodded thoughtfully. 'How about buying them something from the market?'

'I was thinking that they might enjoy going out for a meal.'

'Sounds good. You'll have to find out what they like to eat. Loads of restaurants in Wyckerton,' advised Derek.

'Okay, I will. Will you help me organise it?'

'Guess so,' said Derek, sleepily.

*

It was Saturday. Alfie hadn't seen Nigel since he had blurted out what he had overheard. He went to the shop to help. Nigel didn't seem at all bothered by what he'd been told. Alfie didn't see any point bringing it up again. He still didn't have any proof. It occurred to him to look for the object that Damian needed but he dismissed the idea. He didn't know what it was for a start. If it had been there, Damian wouldn't still be looking for it.

Alfie helped Mary in the shop while it was busy. When most of the customers had been served, he said, 'Mrs Bodley said you've been married for ages.'

Mary smiled. 'I guess we have.'

'Are you going to celebrate your anniversary?'

'We'll give each other a little gift,' she said, 'and have a nice quiet evening listening to Haydn.'

Alfie felt sorry for her. 'If you did eat out, where would you want to go?'

Mary hardly needed to think before she said, 'Scrumptious! It's a wonderful restaurant. I adore eating there.'

Alfie laughed. 'Sounds nice! What sort of food do they serve?'

'Dishes that even I don't know how to make. I'd love to learn their secrets.' She looked fascinated as she recalled their special tastes.

He looked around the shop. 'Shall I go back through and help Nigel. It's really quiet in here now.'

Nigel was preparing the potions for delivery. The row of filled vials grew. Alfie couldn't help thinking that they made a good team, even though he wasn't sure about the importance of each ingredient or the quantities used for different effects.

'I feel as though I'm learning loads from you every week. I'm practising my magic a lot, too,' said Alfie.

'Good. You'll soon be as good as Derek if you carry on practising.'

As if on cue, they heard the shop doorbell jingle. Mary sent Derek through to the workshop.

As Derek entered the room Alfie breathed in sharply, aware that he might have some new information.

'Hello Nigel,' said Derek.

'Well if it isn't Derek. How are you?'

'Fine thanks.' Derek seemed pleased with himself. 'Alfie, we have a surprise for you after supper.'

'What is it?' Alfie didn't know if he could wait.

'Not saying. I promised Bun and Chris. I've only come here to make sure you hurry up with the deliveries.'

'Sounds exciting!' said Nigel. 'It's good that this week's been quiet. Deliveries are minimal.'

'So you won't be too late. I'll let them know.' Derek left via the back door to the garden.

Alfie started to fidget. 'Oh, I just need to ask him something,' he said and ran to catch up. 'Derek!' he shouted to stop him turning up the side path.

Derek turned around and waited.

'Is it about Damian?' asked Alfie.

Derek looked blank for a minute and then his eyes opened wide.

'Oh, no! Sorry, it never occurred to me that you'd think that. It's just something we want to show you.'

Alfie felt deflated.

'Okay. I'll catch up with you later.' He turned back towards the workshop.

As he walked in, Nigel said, 'Can you pop through and help Mary for a while. Loads of non-magics have come in.'

Normally Alfie enjoyed helping to weigh ingredients and serving the customers but he was distracted by Derek's visit. *What are they going to do?*

An hour later he went back to the workshop. Nigel had finished preparing the deliveries.

When the city bell chimed, Nigel looked more relaxed than he did during the day. Mary popped through from the shop.

'Can you take over?' she asked quietly.

'Of course, we've finished in here.' Nigel smiled at her as she left. 'If you want to start the deliveries now, that's fine, I can manage the shop. You don't want to be late back if you're meeting your friends afterwards.'

Alfie hadn't forgotten. 'I wonder what they want to show me?' he said. He wasn't sure he liked surprises. He grabbed the delivery bag and headed towards the door. 'See you next week.'

He felt relieved as he looked at the list. Most of the deliveries were nearby. Thankfully, he didn't have to go to the Northeast Quarter again.

He finished the deliveries quickly and arrived at the B&B with half an hour before supper. He nagged Derek, but he refused to say what he had planned.

When they had eaten, they headed toward the park. Derek was bouncing as he walked.

'Why are we rushing?' Alfie's feet were hardly touching the ground.

'Bun and Chris will be waiting. We've planned a surprise.' Derek looked like a Cheshire cat.

'I don't like surprises. Especially in a magic city. Anything could happen.' Alfie moved his head to one side worriedly.

'It's a good surprise,' said Derek, trying to reassure him.

They went through the park gates and walked until they arrived at the trees on the far side. They thought of it as their area. It was always quiet. No one went there. No one else seemed to know about it. Bun and Chris were already waiting.

'This is what we were planning at school, but you kept trying to find out,' said Derek.

'What?' Alfie was beginning to feel uneasy.

'Derek mentioned that you'd never flown.' Bun seemed amazed at the idea. 'We thought it was about time you did!' He brought a broomstick from behind his back. 'Here, grab hold of this.'

Alfie's stomach jolted. It was the last thing he expected. His arms wouldn't move to take the broom. Bun's face was calm, his eyes were slightly closed. Somehow, his faint smile made Alfie believe in himself. Bun didn't say anything but Alfie took the broom with his clammy hand.

Derek and Chris looked pretty pleased about the idea.

Alfie's hand slid slightly on the worn surface. The broom seemed to make itself comfortable in his grip. *How does this fly?* he wondered. *It's a stick with bristles!* The longer he held it, the less weird the idea of flying became. *Why not? This is what wizards do.* The broom started to feel solid and alive.

He sighed, wishing he could fly for the first time without an audience.

'What happens if I crash into a building or land on a child?' he asked. He remembered how fast the broomsticks flew past when he was with Aunt Edith. 'Or knock over an old lady?'

'You won't. The broom does the work. You just have to stay on,' said Bun.

That could be a problem! 'How do you stay upright?' he asked.

'You just do. Come on, Alfie. I know you can do it. It's really fun. We could start to go places,' said Derek.

Alfie was chuffed by their confidence in him.

'It is really simple. The first time I tried, I just grabbed the broom and jumped on,' said Chris.

'And crashed several times if I remember rightly!' added Bun.

Chris, who never normally needed to prove anything, boasted, 'I'm probably the best broom rider here now!'

'Only because you bounce and don't hurt yourself!' Bun started to laugh.

Alfie watched as they argued. He knew Chris was fearless. He never backed away from a challenge.

Bun seemed worried that Chris's crashes were putting Alfie off. 'You know Chris. He's like a bull in a china shop!' said Bun. 'You'll be fine. You're much more sensible.'

'Thanks,' said Chris, pretending to be offended.

'Let's do it!' said Alfie, holding up the broom.

Chris nodded. 'Stand astride it and grip the neck. If you want to go up, you pull up on the stick. If you want to go down, you push down on it,' he said, looking pretty pleased at his brilliant instructions.

'How much?' asked Alfie.

Chris frowned and looked blank.

'I mean, how hard do I pull or push?'

'Depends how high or low you want it to go.' Chris seemed to think it was a silly question.

Derek interrupted, 'Pretend that you're balancing on a bike. You won't have the pedals to support you, which makes it harder. You know how you lean forward if you want to go faster,' he looked at Alfie, who nodded, 'well, it's sort of the same. If you sit upright you can control the speed until you get used to the feel of the broomstick and get your balance right.'

'Thank you.' Alfie smiled. 'Suppose it's now or never.'

'Good attitude,' said Chris.

Alfie straddled the broom. He placed his hands so that they were comfortable but close to his body. He wanted to sit bolt upright. He bent his elbows and gently pulled his hands towards him. The broom reacted immediately. His weight was supported. He quickly straightened his arms. The broom became inanimate and Alfie relaxed. *Easy!* He bent his arms and the broom hovered a few feet from the ground. He straightened his arms and it became motionless. He had never understood how a broom could be controlled without any handlebars or gears. It was simple. It did what you wanted it to do. He pulled gently and let it float so that his feet were slightly off the ground. He urged it forward and set off at a snail's pace. He lent to the left until it had turned a half-circle. He passed the others on his left, turned again and stopped beside them, still floating.

'Fun, isn't it?' Bun didn't need to say any more.

Alfie wanted to explode. 'It's brilliant! I don't understand how I'm not sliding off sideways. I feel really stable.'

He moved off to do the circuit again but this time he pulled back and went a little bit higher, then floated down to arrive back beside the boys.

'I really want you to be good quickly. It's a pity we only have two brooms with us,' said Derek. 'We could all have flown somewhere.'

'We can do that tomorrow. After the bell tolls, can we fly along the streets?' Alfie's imagination was working overtime.

'If we're careful. We could fly out of the town, as long as we get high enough to be mistaken for birds.' Derek made it seem as if he did it all the time.

'Do you ever get lost?' asked Alfie.

Derek looked at the ground.

'I haven't actually done it very often,' he admitted. 'But Bun and Chris have been to loads of places.'

Alfie could believe that. Maybe parents thought being magic would keep their children safe.

Bun contradicted his thoughts. 'We'd be in deep trouble if our parents found out.' He looked sheepish.

'It's okay if you want to take him flying, Derek,' said Chris. 'We'll wait around here until you get back.'

'And tomorrow we'll all go,' said Bun.

Alfie grinned at them while he hovered above the ground, moving up and down slightly. 'Come on, Derek.'

'Okay, just not too far.' Derek grabbed the other broom and

jumped on, moving off slowly. They climbed gently and flew around the park, smoothly swerving between the trees. It always took ages to walk from the park gates to this area but on brooms it took minutes. They went around the park seven times before Derek took them back to Chris and Bun, who cheered as Alfie landed smoothly.

'Well done! That was a really good landing, I used to come off every time and do a roly-poly!' admitted Chris.

Derek rolled his eyes.

'I think that's enough for today,' said Bun. 'If you push yourself too hard, you'll end up crashing.'

Alfie looked at Bun and wondered if he had been born wise. He sounded like Alfie's father. Today had been very long and very full. Alfie silently agreed and was pleased when they headed home. He wondered what his father would think about this adventure.

CHAPTER THIRTEEN

The Crash Landing

THE next morning Alfie woke up feeling very relaxed. He yawned and stretched his arms above his head, enjoying the fact that it was Sunday. Then he remembered the brooms and wished he could do magic in Wyckerton all day long.

Alfie and Derek took Ernie on an extra long walk and ended up by the river. Ernie stubbornly refused to get his feet wet as he chased the stones they skimmed across the surface.

'Let's see if we can get him to run in,' said Derek, amazed that he stopped just short of the water each time.

'He won't even get stones that only land at the water's edge.' Alfie watched as Ernie ran back and forth from him to the river.

They grinned at each other.

'Come on, Ernie, fetch!' shouted Derek as he wiggled his hand at Ernie before throwing a stone.

Alfie found a stick and threw it into the water. 'Get it!' he encouraged.

They leapt around noisily, but it only excited him. He ran faster but still didn't get his claws wet. Ernie wasn't stupid. His open mouth made him look like a smiling dolphin.

They went back to the B&B and read the books from the study for clues about Nigel. Page after page. They didn't have any luck.

'I can't concentrate any longer,' said Alfie. 'Let's go and find something to eat.'

'Good idea. My sight's gone fuzzy.'

Mrs Bodley was making some sandwiches to tide everyone over until supper.

'You've both been pretty quiet today,' she said.

'We're waiting for the chimes. Alfie rode a broom yesterday!'

Mrs Bodley's eyebrows rose as she acknowledged the achievement. 'Well done!'

'Thank you,' said Alfie, puffing up with pride. 'We can't wait to get back so that I can have another go.' He had just finished speaking when the bell started to toll.

'Please can we take some of these with us to the park?' Derek pointed to the sandwiches and fidgeted.

'I suppose so.' Mrs Bodley normally liked them to sit down when they ate. 'Just this once,' she said. 'There's probably a spare broom in the broom cupboard that you can claim for yourself, Alfie.'

'Thank you!' Alfie left the kitchen and rushed towards the cupboard. 'Which one?' he asked as Derek caught him up.

'Those three are for visitors.' Derek pointed to the three from which he could choose.

The three brooms were completely different. Alfie decided against the largest. It was as tall as his father. The other two were only slightly different in size and were about a foot taller than Alfie. That was where the similarities ended. One was made from a very dark wood with huge, clumpy bristles that started almost halfway up the stick. The other one was a lighter wood, almost golden. It was so well used that it was as shiny as silk. Every ridge and bump was worn smooth. The bristles were made from smaller brushwood and were streamlined. It looked fast. Alfie grinned as he took it out of the cupboard.

Mrs Bodley was watching. 'That's an oak stick. It used to be my brother's,' she said. 'The bristles are willow. Look after him, Derek. From what I remember, this stick's very fast.'

They left the B&B with their broomsticks and marched along the streets. They zigzagged through the other city residents, desperate to get to the park. As they went through the gates Alfie considered jumping on his broom to cross the park quickly, but he had second thoughts. He didn't want to embarrass himself by falling off or crashing into anyone.

Bun and Chris were already there with their brooms. They jumped on them as Alfie moved closer.

'Can you remember what to do?' asked Bun.

'I think so…' said Alfie cautiously.

He carefully slid on and pulled the stick gently towards him. The broom reacted immediately. It creaked slightly as his weight was supported. Bun and Chris flew away. Alfie started to fly before Derek had even jumped on his broom but he soon caught up with Alfie.

'We'll just go up gently and circle so that you can see Wyckerton from the air.'

Alfie could feel the air rush past his head as he looked down at the streets. They had shrunk and looked like a moving map.

Birds flew below him, their wings strong and agile as their feathers moved to let air escape so that they could descend.

Alfie had never felt so free. *I'm like a bird.*

Chris pulled up beside him and grinned. 'You'll soon be good enough to play Manhunt.'

Alfie recalled the riders on brooms shooting past him when he had first arrived in Wyckerton. *Will I ever be that good?*

He laughed as the wind caught Chris's cheek and made it flap. Losing concentration for that second made his broom wobble. The wobble became a sideways wiggle. He had to focus hard to regain control.

Chris and Bun flew around fearlessly. They dived, climbed and zigzagged in front of him, as if they were performing an air show. As they flew around the city, Alfie felt confident enough to try some sharper turns and climbs. His broom responded quickly and he relaxed.

He leant forward to speed up. He'd forgotten about the others and just wanted to see how fast he could go. His hair whipped around and stung his forehead but it added to the feeling of speed. The circuit that they had been following suddenly wasn't enough so he started randomly cutting across the city. He challenged himself to dive and pull up like a rollercoaster.

He felt invincible.

He pulled a sharp turn to the left. He lost his balance and started to tumble out of the sky. The wind gripped his cheek, threatening to rip it off. His stomach muscles went rigid, keeping him bolt upright. As he went over and over, he saw Derek trying to catch him. Then he lost sight of him as he tried to balance out. He stopped tumbling and attempted to pull back on the stick. It slowed down but he still plummeted towards the roofs of buildings. His clammy hands tried to grip the broomstick tighter but it slipped through his fingers. Sweat ran into his eyes. He blinked frantically trying to see.

The best he could do was aim for an alleyway. He hit the ground like a heavyweight boxer. The broom skidded and was left behind as he rolled over again and again along the lane, eventually stopping in a heap outside a shop window.

He was too scared to move. *What if I've broken everything?*

He slowly wiggled his fingers, then gently moved his arms. He was about to lift his head when the shop door was wrenched open and the keeper ran to his side.

'Good grief! Are you alright?' The voice cut through the haze that had started to fill his head. 'Don't move. Let me check you over to see if anything's broken.'

Nothing seemed to hurt. He tried to lift his head again, but it felt too heavy. He could feel the man checking his arms and legs.

'You seem to have been very lucky. Try and sit up slowly. I'll support your head and back.'

The instructions eventually filtered through and Alfie sat up. When he was able to support himself, the man gently tapped his clothes to dust him off.

'I thought I recognised you. You help Nigel in his shop, don't you?'

Alfie focused on the man's face and saw that it was Richard. He tried to speak but started to cough.

'Come on. Let's get you up and into my shop. I think you could do with a cool glass of water.' Richard supported him under the arms and led the way inside.

Alfie sat down on an old chair. 'Thank you,' he whispered, his throat dry.

While Richard went to get some water, Alfie looked around. Everything was old and slightly scruffy. He remembered that Derek had told him that Richard owned an antique shop. His lower lip pulled down as he wondered who would buy stuff like this. The big furniture looked worn out. The smaller ornaments would only suit an old lady's mantelpiece or those huge National Trust houses that his father liked.

He noticed a tall glass case that contained a variety of eggs encrusted with jewels. He didn't like them. About halfway up, on one of the shelves, there was an open box with a glass sphere in it. The little light in the room was shooting off the angles of it. It was much more beautiful than the eggs.

'You look like you're feeling better. Here you are,' said Richard, holding out a glass of water.

'Thank you.' Alfie took it and gulped it down. It cleared out some of the dust that had caught in his throat.

'I think it might be best if you walk home. It's even difficult for an expert to take off in a street this narrow.' Richard smiled.

Richard looked a lot better than he had when he'd seen him in Nigel's shop. He was certainly more willing to talk.

'You'll probably ache tomorrow. If you do, pop in and see Nigel. He enjoys keeping everyone as healthy as himself.'

Alfie slumped as he remembered that Nigel's health was in danger.

Richard frowned. 'What's wrong?' he asked, encouragingly.

Alfie found it hard to keep his worries bottled up. 'I overheard someone saying that they wanted Nigel to die.'

Richard looked horrified.

'What! Do you have any idea who it was?' His voice was low and hard.

'No.' Alfie didn't mention Damian, as he knew Nigel disapproved of Alfie blaming him.

Richard rubbed his chin. 'Nigel's a good man. You probably

heard incorrectly.' He shook his head in disbelief and then smiled. 'Anyway, do you think you'll survive the walk home or would you like me to come with you?'

The doorbell rattled. Then the door thudded and crashed open. Derek rushed in.

'We couldn't find you! Your broomstick is right at the other end of the lane. I thought you'd disintegrated!' He looked really scared.

Richard laughed gently. 'He's okay. We were just discussing getting home. Now you've arrived, I reckon he's in good hands.'

Derek took a deep breath and puffed it out with relief.

'He will be. We'll be walking back!' He wasn't taking any more risks.

Alfie was pleased. He coughed gently to relieve his dry throat. 'It's going to take something major to get me on a broom again.'

They walked out of the shop slowly. Alfie looked up as he heard applause. Bun and Chris were standing outside, clapping and cheering.

'After that fall, I thought we'd be carrying you home!' said Chris.

'Luckily your broom survived, too.' Bun was holding a broom in each hand. It was obvious which one was Alfie's from the amount of dirt ground into the bristles.

Alfie ached as he walked along the dark streets. He wiggled his nose to dislodge the dust stuck up his nostrils. Even swallowing was difficult with his mouth caked in dirt. Slowly, he changed his mind about not flying again. Crashing had been his fault; he always pushed himself too hard.

Anyway, walking took too long. He'd managed to crash on the opposite side of town in the Northeast Quarter. If he crashed again, he was going to make sure he did it closer to the B&B!

CHAPTER FOURTEEN

Smoky Potion

AS usual, Alfie ran down the stone staircase and slid down the two wooden banister rails. Pippa watched enviously. She wasn't quite tall enough to climb onto them yet. Alfie landed skilfully at the foot of the stairs on his way to the kitchen to get some biscuits. He couldn't wait until supper.

As he opened the kitchen door he saw that Mrs Bodley was already cooking. He faltered before she saw him. Would she mind that he was always eating? He carried on regardless.

He walked behind Mrs Bodley and glanced over her right shoulder. Floating around in front of her was a recipe written in the air.

He did a double-take. 'How did you do that?'

'What?' She turned to look at him.

'That!' He pointed to the words.

'It's a recipe.' She didn't seem to know why he was pointing at it.

'But how is it floating in mid-air? It's not even on paper.' He couldn't believe that she thought it was normal.

'Oh. It's from a cookery book over there on the shelf. It saves me having to find the page.' She spoke as if it was perfectly natural.

Alfie watched the words float steadily around. Mesmerised, his question came out slowly, 'Is it easy?'

Mrs Bodley laughed.

'You just summon up the thing you want by imagining it, point at the correct book and swirl your hand around like this…' She moved a relaxed hand in a circle twice, then flicked it and said,

'*Memorium.*' A second recipe appeared. 'You have to have read it before, of course.'

Alfie was amazed. He copied her movements and said the word. Nothing happened.

'You have to be familiar with what you're trying to see. You couldn't just walk around with pages floating beside you,' she said, as if it was obvious.

'It has to be something that you already know and want to use?' asked Alfie.

'Exactly.' She seemed pleased that she had explained it so well. 'Did you come in for anything in particular?'

Alfie remembered why he was in the kitchen. 'I was hungry. I came down for some biscuits.'

'That's fine as long as you take some fruit as well. By *take*, I mean *eat*. I don't want to find it rotting in your room in a few days.' She smiled at him. 'I'll be starting supper soon. Don't fill yourself up…' her voice petered out as she realised that Alfie would always be able to eat.

Alfie walked over to the larder door. He wondered what percentage of fruit to biscuits he'd get away with. He reached up to get the biscuit tin and took a handful. As he replaced it he saw a door in the corner of the larder.

'I've never noticed that other door in there,' he said as he walked back into the kitchen.

Mrs Bodley looked confused and then said, 'Ah, that goes down to the cellar. I expect in earlier times they used it to store food to keep it cool.' She carried on baking.

'Thanks for the biscuits.'

Alfie ran up the stairs and into the bedroom.

'Come on, Derek. We only have a couple of hours until supper.'

'Where are we going?'

Alfie sighed. 'To book the restaurant for Nigel and Mary. *And* convince him to take her out,' he said, almost as an afterthought.

Derek jumped up from his bed. They rushed downstairs and out of the front door, the biscuits already eaten.

It didn't take them as long to get to Nigel's as it did to convince him to take Mary out.

'I've already bought her a lovely gift.'

'But lady's like to eat out.' Alfie didn't actually know if it was true.

Nigel laughed and said, 'You know that from experience, I suppose?' He looked at the two eager faces in front of him. 'Okay, you win. I'll have to finish making potions and tidy up before I go, though.' He looked around at the mess.

Alfie felt chuffed as he looked around the room. 'It's not as neat as we keep it on Saturdays!' he said.

'That's true, but I've been busy today.' Nigel smiled at him. Alfie knew he was pretending that he'd worked harder than they did on Saturdays.

'We'll come back later and tidy up. I know where everything goes now,' offered Alfie.

'That would be a great help, especially as I'm being forced to go out!' said Nigel. Alfie and Derek laughed as Nigel pulled a face at them.

Alfie and Derek reached the restaurant just as the third strike of the city bell faded away. They approached the headwaiter that was standing by his diary of bookings.

'Please can we book a table for two this evening?' Alfie was chuffed that they'd convinced Nigel to take Mary to her favourite restaurant, Scrumptious.

'Of course,' said the headwaiter. 'What time would you prefer?'

Alfie looked at Derek who shrugged.

'Half-past eight, please,' he said.

'Perfect, what name?'

They looked at each other again.

'Nigel and Mary,' they said in unison.

The headwaiter smiled, not wanting to point out that he usually took a surname. 'That's all booked,' he said.

They headed to the B&B for supper before going to help Nigel tidy his shop. As they walked into the entrance hall, Mr Bodley was heading towards the kitchen.

'Suffer is ready!' he announced and pulled a face at them.

'Oh no!' whispered Derek. 'You have to avoid Mum's shepherd's pie. It's vile. The code word is *suffer*, instead of *supper*. It's a good job Dad's on our side.'

The smells had found their way to the entrance hall. Alfie raced towards the kitchen, unaware of Derek's warning. His stomach groaned as he waited for everyone to be seated.

No one ever seemed to be as hungry as he was. They dawdled into the kitchen and the table adjusted to seat them. Alfie locked his fingers together so that he didn't dive in first. Aunt Edith started to serve herself. Relieved, Alfie quickly followed.

He picked up a big serving spoon and reached towards the minced meat and potato dish. He lowered it, intending to fill his plate. The spoon dived off sideways and missed, gently hitting the tabletop. *How did that happen?* He tried again. This time the spoon swung off to the right, chinking the water jug. He clenched his jaw and held the spoon tightly as he prepared for a third go. He spotted Derek concentrating on the serving spoon.

Derek leant toward him and whispered, '*Not* the shepherd's pie!'

Alfie looked at Mr Bodley. He moved his eyes towards the shepherd's pie and grimaced.

Alfie turned back to Derek and whispered, 'But everything Mrs Bodley makes is delicious.' He hesitated over the dish, wondering if it was another one of Mr Bodley's jokes.

'Don't say I didn't warn you!' said Derek.

Alfie looked around the table. He wondered if the guests had heard Derek. They were helping themselves to fish pie and whispering to each other.

Alfie couldn't chance it. He moved the spoon over to the fish pie and scooped some onto his plate. As he looked up, Aunt Edith winked at him.

When everyone's dish was empty Mrs Bodley said, 'Ah, no one's had any shepherd's pie. Alfie, you will, won't you? You usually have seconds.' She looked across at him.

He felt his nostrils start to close as his nose wrinkled up. He stopped himself just in time. 'Umm…' The word strung out, reluctantly. 'Can I try a little taste?'

Mrs Bodley smiled and piled a huge spoonful onto his plate.

'Anyone else?' She looked around but they all shook their heads, including Mr Locksley.

Alfie put a tiny bit on his fork and slowly opened his mouth. His body shuddered as the taste spread across his tongue. Lifting his glass he gulped down the water, taking the food with it. He put his knife and fork down neatly.

'I'm sorry, I'm too full.' He hoped his face didn't show his disgust. He couldn't relax his muscles. He was sure his lips were pulled back, baring his teeth.

Alfie could see tears glistening in Derek's eyes as he tried to keep a straight face. Mr Bodley had his hand over his mouth. His shoulders were shaking.

'That's a shame.' She offered the pie around again. No one took any. 'I don't think I'll bother making this again. It's never eaten,' she said as she carried it towards the sink.

Alfie was relieved that Mrs Bodley didn't turn around to see Derek doing a victory dance as everyone else grinned, including Aunt Edith.

Pudding was apple pie and custard. It was warm and sweet, making the memory of the shepherd's pie disappear. He held the creamy custard in his mouth, pushing it between his teeth. Alfie tidied his dish, thankful that he didn't have to wash-up.

They rushed out of the B&B and hurried along the street towards Nigel's shop. When they arrived, they tried the shop door but it was already locked. They made their way around the back to the workshop.

As they went in, Nigel smiled at them. 'It became really busy. Mary's upstairs getting ready. I'm running late, I'm sure the restaurant won't mind, though.' He was tidying up as he spoke.

'We can finish clearing up,' said Alfie. 'I know where everything goes and Derek can help. We'll lock up when we've finished.'

Nigel frowned his frustration as he remembered the burglary.

Shaking his head, he mumbled, 'I can't see what anyone would want from a potion shop...'

Alfie regretted reminding him about it.

'You get ready. We'll finish here.'

Nigel looked down at his cloak and pretended to be offended. 'I am ready. Mary loves me anyway,' he sounded confident but his forehead slowly wrinkled. 'Maybe I should make an effort. I'll change my cloak,' he said. 'Right, the shop is tidy and locked, so it's just the mess in here. I'll be off then. Bye.' He didn't wait for a reply.

Alfie and Derek stood in the empty workshop.

'So where do we start?' asked Derek.

'Well...' Alfie had helped Nigel so many times he'd felt sure that he would be fine on his own. 'Um...' He looked around at the used bottles of ingredients. 'The bottles have numbers etched in the glass.' He showed Derek the bottle that he'd picked up. 'They go on the shelves in numerical order.'

'That seems easy.' Derek started to turn each bottle around so that its number was facing them.

'Good idea.' Alfie joined in. It didn't take long before all the bottles were back on the shelves. They stood admiring their work.

'What about this one? It doesn't have a number?'

'Oh.' Alfie looked at the bottle. 'Just leave it on the bench. Nigel can deal with it tomorrow.'

They put the unused delivery vials back on the shelf. Nigel had left an untidy pile of paperwork, which they put in neat stacks. They made sure the cupboard doors and drawers were tightly shut.

'Good job!' said Derek, when he thought they'd finished.

'I think the cauldrons will need cleaning. Just empty out any bits left in the bottom and then we're finished.' Alfie grabbed a dirty cauldron and took it over to the sink.

Derek turned to help. As he grabbed the handle of the cauldron that was on the burner, a huge cloud of white smoke rose from it.

Derek jumped away. 'What on earth...?' he said.

Alfie turned to look, his pulse quickened. 'We have to stop it burning down the workshop!' He took a step toward the cauldron.

An image formed in the smoke. Alfie looked at Derek to make sure he wasn't imagining it. He was relieved to see Derek standing open-mouthed, staring at the smoke.

'Does that usually happen?' squeaked Derek.

In the smoke a man appeared. Alfie recognised him. He was holding a necklace that looked solid enough to touch. Blue stones hung from the gold chain. The man faded. The necklace grew to fill the smoke before the image changed to Nigel. He clutched his chest, as if he was dying from a heart attack. The smoke collapsed back into the cauldron and they looked at each other.

Alfie found his voice first, 'Did you see that!'

Derek nodded, still stunned. 'Was that Mr Locksley?' he squeaked.

'Yes. When he arrived at the B&B I saw him with *that* necklace.'

'Are you sure?'

Alfie thought back to what Damian had said in the Northeast Quarter. 'I think that necklace is the thing that Damian needs.'

'We have to find Mr Locksley,' said Derek.

'Damian said that Nigel is the only one who can destroy it. We have to get it. Then Nigel can break it, before Damian uses it against him.' He hadn't ever felt this positive. They *could* actually end this before Nigel was harmed.

A shuffling sound outside caught Alfie's attention. He ran over to the door and out into the garden. He looked along the path towards the street. Nothing there.

A street lamp lit a dark shape. Alfie gasped and ran towards the street, skidding to a halt as he tried to see where the figure had gone. No one was there. *They couldn't have moved fast enough to be out of sight,* he thought, doubting himself.

As he turned back towards the passageway, Derek was there.

'What was it?' he asked.

'I thought I saw someone but now I'm not sure.' said Alfie. 'Did you see anything?'

'No, I'm not sharp-eyed like you are. I didn't even hear anything,' admitted Derek.

'There was no one in the street. I managed to get there pretty fast. It must have been a cat or something.' He wrinkled his chin, feeling sure he'd seen someone but it wasn't possible. 'Come on. Let's finish tidying up.'

Irritated that they might have been watched, Alfie clenched his teeth as he cleaned out the cauldrons.

He looked at Derek who was putting a clean cauldron on the bench. 'We have to finish here and get that necklace from Mr Locksley. Nigel will know how to destroy it.' Alfie couldn't shake off the feeling that things were getting desperate.

When they had finished, Alfie stood in the doorway. He made sure everything was in its place. He closed the door and locked it.

They raced back to the B&B to find Mr Locksley. They looked everywhere and ended up in the sitting room.

'What on earth are you doing, rushing around like lunatics?' Mrs Bodley had followed them from the kitchen.

'Do you know where Mr Locksley is?' Alfie didn't realise that he was shouting.

'Shh, you'll wake Aunt Edith.' Mrs Bodley kept her voice low.

Alfie looked over to Aunt Edith's chair, a little baffled that she always fell asleep in a public place. 'But do you know?' he whispered.

'He was supposed to leave earlier, but his train was cancelled. He's gone to bed. He's leaving very early tomorrow.'

'Oh no. He mustn't leave until we've seen him,' said Derek. He headed toward the door.

'No, you don't!' Mrs Bodley sounded so severe he stopped in his tracks. 'You will *not* disturb the guests. I'll tell him in the morning that you were looking for him.'

Alfie opened his mouth to argue but when he saw Mrs Bodley's face, he didn't have the nerve to speak. He would just have to be up and ready to catch Mr Locksley before he left in the morning.

CHAPTER FIFTEEN

The Necklace

THE noise as the mini-hammer slammed against the two bells of the alarm clock would have woken the dead. Alfie reached out sleepily but his hand couldn't find the clock or the button on the top that turned it off. Derek groaned. Alfie sighed. He wondered why he had put the clock on the dresser on the other side of the room.

His body felt weak and his eyes grainy as he stumbled over and hit the clock hard. *Stupid clock!* As he headed back towards his bed, a thought struggled to escape the fuggy cloud in his head. As it disappeared, he became fully awake.

'Derek, come on, get up! We have to catch Mr Locksley.' He saw Derek look at the clock.

'It's five o'clock.' Derek's covers muffled his voice.

'I know.' Alfie slung on his dressing gown and wrestled his feet into his slippers. 'I don't know what time he's leaving.'

Derek slid one leg out of the covers so that it hung over the edge of his bed, making his foot barely visible. 'I'm up, I'm up,' he mumbled.

Alfie didn't want to waste time chivvying him along. 'I'm going down to the kitchen. You catch up.'

He opened the bedroom door to darkness and wondered if five o'clock was a bit early. He silently went down the narrow brick stairs. As he neared the bottom of the wooden steps, he could hear mumbling. He turned at the bottom step, relieved that the kitchen light was showing under the door.

Mrs Bodley looked up as he entered. She looked tired but still managed to smile.

'Good morning, Alfie, I was just explaining to Mr Locksley that you were anxious to see him,' she said.

Alfie looked at Mr Locksley as he tucked into a huge breakfast of bacon and eggs.

'Um... did you ever have a necklace with blue stones in it?'

Mr Locksley's head shot up, the remains of the food in his mouth splattered. 'Yes! Have you found it?'

Alfie's thoughts stalled as he realised what Mr Locksley had said.

He gasped, 'You mean you don't have it anymore?' *Why did I think that this was going to be easy?*

'Afraid not. I dropped it a couple of days after I bought it from the antique shop, Slightly Shabby. The shop owner gave me a good deal after I told him I was staying here.' He looked like he was remembering. 'Shame too. I was going to take it to my mother in Ireland. The shop owner was interested in that fact. He said he'd always wanted to go there. She likes blue, my mother. Not that it was cheap...' He rambled on, but Alfie wasn't listening.

How on earth am I going to find it now? he wondered.

Derek appeared at the kitchen door.

'Does he have it?' asked Derek. Alfie shook his head. 'So what will we do now?'

Alfie really didn't know. He hit the side of his head with the heel of his hand to wake up his tired brain.

'Would you two like breakfast now?' asked Mrs Bodley.

Alfie felt glum as they both sat down. Mrs Bodley placed full plates of crispy bacon and scrambled egg in front of them.

Mr Locksley chatted away until it was time for him to leave. 'Well, I'd best be off. Don't want to miss the train.' He stood up and moved off at a snail's pace, finding his large body difficult to manoeuvre. Mrs Bodley politely went with him to the front door.

Alfie munched away at his breakfast but didn't feel any better with a full stomach.

'We were so close. All the signs pointed to that necklace. It could be anywhere,' he said.

Derek breathed out noisily through his nose.

It was barely six o'clock when they went back upstairs and rested on their beds. Derek's breathing soon became regular and Alfie guessed that he'd gone back to sleep. He lay wide-awake as his head buzzed with useless information.

*

They walked to school silently. Neither of them had any answers. Alfie didn't see the point of going over it again.

Luckily the first lesson was double English. Mr Kalm was already sitting at his big desk when they entered the room. As usual, his cardigan was buttoned up incorrectly and his beige corduroy trousers were baggy.

'We are going to start reading one of three books.' He told the class the titles and briefly explained what they were about. 'I have decided to let you choose. Can you write a brief explanation about the one you wish to read and why. The best piece of work will decide which book we read.'

Passing notes wasn't a problem. Mr Kalm hardly ever moved from his chair. Alfie waggled his pen at Bun to get his attention. He dropped the rolled-up note on the floor and flicked it with his foot. Alfie explained about the necklace and Mr Locksley. The messages went back and forth:

Bun: Do you know where he lost it?

Alfie: No, but he bought it from Richard's shop.

Bun: We could go and ask Richard. Maybe someone found it and took it back.

Alfie: We could try…

Bun: I'll tell Chris.

Alfie looked across the room at Bun and half-smiled. They both knew that it would probably be a waste of time asking Richard.

Derek kicked Alfie under the desk. As Alfie turned around, Derek nodded towards the front of the classroom. Mr Kalm had started to walk around the classroom as he talked. Alfie moved his book so that it looked like he was writing and knocked the rolled-up note off his desk and onto the floor. It bounced out of reach. He looked up. Mr Kalm was getting closer. Alfie slid down in his chair and stretched out his foot but still couldn't reach it. Mr Kalm was inches away. Alfie watched as Jazz bent down and scooped up the paper.

'You dropped your pen, Alfie,' she said loudly, and very obviously passed him a pen, carefully including the note.

'Thank you.' He smiled gratefully.

Their third lesson was maths. Miss Lloyd watched them with her keen eyes. She liked silence during her lesson. She had written out some long division problems on the blackboard and expected them to work through them. Alfie was still on the first one. He didn't have the energy to complete them. He was still tired from waking so early. He knew that Miss Lloyd would give him something else to do if he finished them. She glanced at her watch.

'Finish these for your homework,' she said, and left abruptly as the bell signalled break-time.

Alfie stayed at his desk, unable to get up and go outside. He lowered his head onto his folded arm. He barely heard the girls at the desk in front of him talking. They stood up and walked towards the door.

'So what will you do with it?'

'I ought to find the owner, but it's so beautiful. The blue goes with my eyes. I just want to keep it.'

'You can't! Whoever lost it must be distraught.'

Their voices faded as they went through the door, 'How could anyone not notice losing a necklace that heavy?'

Alfie's eyes were closed. He could easily have fallen asleep. Something made him register the parting words. Heavy. Yes, his eyes were heavy…. He sat bolt upright when the other words finally filtered through. As he stood up, his legs straightened and knocked his chair so hard it fell backwards. He ran out into the corridor but it was empty. Who were they? He hadn't recognised their voices.

He felt panic rising in his throat. He'd never discover who they were. He took slow, deep breaths. He tried to think logically, *We've just finished a maths lesson. Which girls are in my set?*

He really didn't know. He couldn't wait until the next maths lesson tomorrow. He had to find them now. He went back into the classroom.

Derek was picking up his chair. 'Why did you rush off?'

'Did you notice those two girls sitting at the desk in front of us?'

Derek looked at him oddly.

'Why would I do that?' he asked, as if it were a rude question.

'I *mean* do you know who they were?'

'Jane and Sarah,' said Derek, rather too quickly. Then his cheeks went pink.

'So you can find them? Good.' Alfie started to move towards the door. 'Come on,' he said impatiently as Derek hadn't moved.

'Where?' Derek didn't know what was happening. 'Why?'

'They've found a necklace…' Alfie started to explain. He had to run to catch up as Derek sprinted out of the room.

They didn't have much time left to look. As they ran, they scanned the tuck-shop queue, then along the passageways between the classrooms, bobbing up to look inside each room. They were about to go into the assembly hall when the end of break bell peeled into the air telling them that they would have to leave it until lunchtime.

'We have double science now. Are they in our class?' asked Alfie.

'No. We're split into smaller groups. I don't think we have another class with them today.'

Alfie found it difficult to concentrate during the lesson. The bitter smells of the science room were horrible compared with the fragrant ones at Nigel's shop. He tapped the test tubes with a pencil as he rested his chin on the long wooden bench. The warm, stuffy room made it even harder to stay awake.

The fresh air felt good as they left the classroom. Bun and Chris joined them as they walked to the canteen. Alfie looked around as he entered but realised he wouldn't recognise the two girls even if they were there. He noticed Derek scan the room, too.

'They're not in here,' Derek informed him.

Alfie nodded. 'We'll eat. Then find them.'

As usual their lunch trays were packed with hot food. Alfie

stuffed his pockets with biscuits for later. They sat down at one of the round tables.

'Where do girls go at break times?' asked Alfie. He didn't have a clue. He knew that lots of the boys played football on the sports field.

The others looked puzzled.

'Don't know.' Bun shook his head.

'We'll have to look in the places that we don't usually go.' Chris smiled as if he'd come up with a master plan.

When they'd cleared away their trays, they started their assault on the school grounds. They found Martha and Jazz but they were with other girls from the city. They couldn't help locate Jane and Sarah.

It took half the lunch break to find them. Alfie sighed with relief as Derek pointed at two girls sitting on a low wall, surrounded by loads of other girls. He didn't flinch as he walked through the circle. He approached the two that Derek had indicated and explained about the lost necklace.

'How do we know you didn't just overhear us?' asked Jane.

'If I can describe it, will you let me have it?' said Alfie.

Reluctantly, she nodded.

When he finished she was impressed.

'You must be telling the truth. I've never told anyone the clasp is a lizard's head. I'll bring it in tomorrow.'

'Could we come and collect it this evening? The owner is leaving today,' Alfie lied. He couldn't explain to non-magics that the necklace had to be destroyed by a wizard to stop him from dying. He doubted that she would believe him anyway.

'Sure, but I live in Upper Weston.' She told him the address. 'It's quite a way from Wyckerton. Will your parents bring you?'

'I'm not sure,' Alfie pretended to think about it. 'We'll probably get there after dark.' He knew exactly how they were going to get there, but he could hardly tell her.

As they walked away, Derek whispered, 'Broomsticks?'

'Of course,' said Alfie, smiling at him. He was already looking forward to this evening's adventure.

*

Alfie's nerves jangled as Derek kept looking over his shoulder later that evening when they left the B&B with their broomsticks. It was normal for the youngsters of the city to go to the park and practise magic together.

'Stop it,' said Alfie.

'I can't help it. If Mum catches us, we'll be for the high jump.'

Alfie knew that Mrs Bodley would disapprove if she found out they had left the city. 'How will she find out? She never follows us.'

'Maybe Mum's a witch?' said Derek.

They both burst out laughing.

'You've been spending too much time with non-magics,' said Alfie.

They stopped laughing, realising that they probably wouldn't survive Mrs Bodley's wrath if she discovered what they were about to do.

Alfie tried not to think about it. Derek told him that anyone who left the city always climbed high enough to avoid being seen from the outside, before making their move away from the protective walls. Alfie pretended he was already flying. His nerves started to settle down.

They met Bun and Chris at their usual spot on the far side of the park. Chris seemed really excited as he waited impatiently.

'You're going to be amazed by this, Alfie. There's nothing as exciting as flying high over the countryside at night.' Chris was actually fidgeting as he talked. 'Except Manhunt,' he added as an afterthought.

Alfie was only concerned with getting the necklace back. He hadn't thought about the flight.

'Best of all is the freedom. It's a huge place out there,' continued Chris.

'How do we find our way back?' Alfie felt worried and looked at Derek.

'We're not going too far,' Derek assured him. 'Wyckerton is quite well lit…' he said, stating the obvious.

'Oh yeah,' said Alfie. 'Guess I'm ready!' He jumped onto his broomstick, amazed that his stomach was calm.

'We'll meet you outside the city. It's best if we leave in pairs,' said Bun. He zoomed off with Chris. They disappeared almost immediately.

Alfie followed Derek. He knew the park and the best area to slip out and over the wall. They whizzed around the perimeter and flew higher and higher. The air buffeted against Alfie's face, making whooping sounds. His hair stung his eyes. He didn't care. There wasn't another feeling on earth like flying.

He felt his blood pumping through his veins. He understood why Chris had been so excited. He flew faster to catch up with Derek. He was about to overtake when Derek slid over the wall to the outside world.

Alfie's speed made it hard to follow. He jerked the handle to the right. He didn't want to lose sight of Derek. He descended as he snaked from side to side and almost lost control. A huge tree loomed ahead as he fought to regain his balance. He pulled the handle to climb, just avoiding the top of the tree and flinched as a thin branch scratched his cheek. Fighting to go in a straight line, he climbed even higher to avoid being seen.

'Are you all right? Sorry, I thought you'd be okay with that manoeuvre.' Derek looked concerned as he re-joined him.

'I would have been, but I forgot we were leaving and started racing you.' Alfie laughed with relief.

'Racing me?' Derek looked dumbfounded. 'We are on a mission!'

'I know. I'll concentrate now,' said Alfie, cross with himself.

Derek shook his head as Bun and Chris joined them. They'd obviously seen what Alfie had done. They were both laughing.

Bun chose their course and flew off gently towards a tiny speck of lights in the distance. 'That's Upper Weston. It won't take too long to fly there. We'll have to stop outside the village and walk the rest of the way,' he said.

They didn't speed up and Alfie was pleased. The crisp, night air felt cool and clean. The view stretched out around him. Hedges divided the green mass below so it looked like stamps laid out on a tabletop. Everything was held in a huge bowl, its sides made from hills and mountains.

Alfie's shirt billowed under his cloak as the air rushed in and touched his skin. It tickled. He smiled, amazed at what he was doing. Chris came up beside him and pointed down to get his attention. Alfie's gaze followed the line of Chris's arm. He saw a white owl gliding just below them. Its wings suddenly folded in as it dived to catch its prey.

Far too quickly, Bun started to descend. They landed beside a large cluster of trees.

'The broomsticks will be fine here,' said Derek as he tucked his between some branches until it was almost invisible. He took Alfie's and hid it.

'What if we can't find them?' Alfie didn't fancy the long walk home.

'Don't worry. They won't get lost.' Chris tapped his nose.

'Make sure you hide yours properly, Chris. Someone nearly found it last time,' said Bun, raising his eyebrows.

'I know, I know,' said Chris as he double-checked.

Alfie glanced back at the tree as they walked off. He tried to memorise something significant about it but all the leafless trees looked the same. The broomsticks had completely disappeared. He hoped they would be able to find them again.

Just as they were about to leave the cover of the trees, Bun removed his cloak. It immediately shrunk into a handkerchief.

'We can't arrive looking like wizards,' he said as the others removed theirs too.

They walked to the address Jane had given them. It was a welcoming house on a quiet road. The lights shone on the porch. Alfie rang the doorbell. Jane answered almost immediately and invited them into the hallway. Chris and Bun opted to wait outside. After Derek and Alfie had entered, she closed the door to shut in the heat of the hall.

'Wait here. I left it upstairs just in case you didn't come.' She looked disappointed. Alfie felt guilty for a split-second. She came back down carrying a small bag. 'I've put it in here to keep it safe. I hope the man's pleased to get it back.' She handed him the bag after taking a quick look. 'It really is beautiful.'

Alfie peeped into the bag. His heart missed a beat. He had Mr Locksley's necklace. His cold fingers turned numb as he held the handles of the bag firmly, worried that Jane would change her mind.

'Thank you, I know that he'll be grateful,' he said as they left. He carefully put the small bag into his trouser pocket.

All the way back to the woods Alfie worried that they wouldn't find their broomsticks. When they arrived back at the copse, they put on their cloaks. Alfie was glad of the warmth. He didn't recognise anything. None of the trees stood out. They were all disguised as each other. They were going to be wandering around for hours.

He jumped at the shrill whistle Derek let out and turned to him, scowling. He was just about to moan when Bun and Chris also made short, sharp whistles. Three broomsticks floated down towards them.

'Blimey, that's brilliant!' Alfie grinned. 'They responded to your whistle.'

'It only works if they're within hearing distance,' Derek informed him.

Even though he understood what Derek had meant, he giggled as a vision of a broom with ears popped into his head.

'You have to get yours to come down,' said Derek.

Alfie put his lips together and blew. Nothing came out except air. He tried again but as they were watching him, he couldn't whistle. He began to panic that he'd have to walk back to Wyckerton.

Chris started to laugh. 'Looks like it's the end of your broom-flying career!' he said unhelpfully.

Bun puffed up his cheeks to stop himself laughing. Derek turned his back on Alfie, but he could see his shoulders wobbling.

'Can you whistle?' asked Chris, his smile was so big his white teeth showed up in the moonlight.

'I can normally. You're all putting me off!' said Alfie.

He took a deep breath and tried again. He managed a feeble

noise and the broom floated towards him. He let out a huge sigh of relief as he jumped on.

'I would say let's race back but you don't know the safest way into the city without being seen. We'll save that for next time.' Derek jumped onto his broom and whizzed into the air. Bun and Chris went next, leaving Alfie to follow.

The sights below plus the wind in his face left Alfie breathless. They descended as they approached the city wall. Alfie looked down and saw rabbits hopping around. As they lolloped along, their white tails flashed at any eagle-eyed predators.

They slowed down and hovered outside the city wall, knowing they could still be spotted on their way back into Wyckerton.

'There are still loads of people around. We'll have to go high and circle down slowly. That way they'll think we've been here all the time. Word won't get back to Mum that we left the city.' Derek looked at Alfie.

He nodded his agreement. Derek pulled his broomstick back and climbed vertically until he was happy with the height. They followed. The sound as his broom whooshed through the silent air was like music. They slowly edged into the city and descended as if they'd been there all the time.

They jumped off as they landed. Alfie attempted to run so he could get to Nigel's quickly but Chris grabbed his arm.

'Give me your broomstick. You'll be able to get there quicker if you don't have to carry it.'

'Thanks.' Alfie handed over his broom.

He called back over his shoulder as he started to run, 'I'll let you know how Nigel destroys this.' He held up the bag containing the necklace and grinned.

He ran, knowing that Nigel's life depended on him. It was a relief to eventually see the park gates. Derek caught up with him as he left the park. They headed along the wide streets.

Even though he was breathless, Alfie couldn't help speaking, 'I can't wait to watch Nigel destroy this. It's amazing to think that we've foiled the plan to kill him.' Alfie looked over at Derek and grinned.

He didn't stand a chance as his foot caught in a loose paving slab. He fell downward at the same speed he had been moving forward. He hit the ground with a thump.

Derek stopped and ran back the few steps needed to lift Alfie. He'd hit his chin on the ground and blood was running down his neck. Derek handed him a handkerchief to stop the bleeding. Alfie grabbed it and shoved it on his chin.

'I'M FINE!' he shouted. 'Let's just get over to Nigel's.'

'Is the necklace okay?' asked Derek.

'Of course it is,' Alfie opened the bag and held it out so that Derek could look in. 'Only Nigel can break it. See…'

Derek gasped. He looked at Alfie, confusion on his face.

Alfie frowned. 'What…?' He looked into the bag and saw the shattered necklace. 'But… that's not possible.' He sunk on to the pavement, his eyes unfocused. Blood still trickled from his chin. He looked at Derek, unwilling to admit what the broken necklace meant.

'You're not hurt again, are you?' asked a familiar voice.

Alfie looked up into the face of Richard and slowly nodded his head.

'I always seem to find you injured on a street.' Richard started to laugh but stopped when they didn't join in. 'Anything else wrong?'

'We thought we had something to save Nigel. We've broken it and it shouldn't have broken. That means it wasn't even the right object,' explained Derek. He seemed to know that Alfie wasn't going to speak.

'Oh … can I see?'

Derek took the bag from Alfie and opened it to show Richard.

'That's a great pity.' Richard seemed more disappointed than either of them.

Alfie looked up at him and frowned. He didn't feel like being polite.

'We should go. I have blood on my clothes.' He jumped up and vaguely smiled.

As they moved out of earshot, Derek said, 'What on earth are we going to do now?'

Alfie felt defeated. 'I don't know,' he said quietly.

CHAPTER SIXTEEN

Alice

THE snow fell gently on Christmas day, covering everything in a glistening blanket of white. Christmas lights flickered above the shops. Non-magics came into Wyckerton to see the decorations. All the shops were closed. Snowmen of all shapes and sizes filled the streets, some completed, others half-built. Three young children struggled to lift a ball of snow onto a larger one. Alfie and Derek went over to help plonk the head on the body and finish the snowman.

'There you go,' said Derek.

'Thanks.' The young boy smiled and then jumped behind the snowman as Alfie was hit in the neck by a snowball. The freezing icicles warmed as they touched his skin and dribbles of icy water ran inside his collar.

'Oi!' he shouted as he turned to see Chris duck behind a large snowman. 'That's not big enough to hide you.' Alfie bent down and gathered some snow, ran past Chris and pelted him straight in the face.

Bun jumped out with an armful of balls and bombarded Alfie; throwing them one after another. Derek came to his rescue as the smaller children joined in. They all used the snowmen as cover, darting out from behind them to attack.

The four boys walked back to the B&B. Alfie blew into his hands to warm them.

'I'm freezing.'

'Me too,' said Derek.

'You need some of these WarmDrys,' said Bun. 'They're waterproof and warm.'

Alfie looked at Bun and Chris's gloves. They looked bone dry. He inwardly smiled, happy that Mrs Bodley had suggested Alfie buy a pair for Derek's Christmas present.

'I can't wait to have Christmas lunch. Mrs Bodley lays on the best spread,' said Chris, rubbing his stomach.

Alfie felt a warm glow as they walked through the front door of the B&B. The decorated tree stood in the entrance hall. It reached up two storeys. Christmas carols rang out as the tree baubles finished singing, "The Twelve Days of Christmas". As each gift was mentioned, mini-models of them sang their own part. Leaping lords, milk maids, gold rings, humming birds and a partridge in a pear tree popped up and disappeared all over the huge tree. Alfie had already tried to touch the star from the top of the second staircase. They followed the cheery noise from the kitchen and went in to join everyone. There were only a few guests staying but Nigel, Mary, Chris's parents and Bun's parents had joined them. The table had expanded to seat everyone but grew as the four boys approached.

Alfie had never seen a turkey as large as the one steaming in the centre of the table. It was surrounded by dishes of vegetables, crispy roast potatoes and rich gravy. He sat down next to Derek as the turkey was carved. Aunt Edith served herself and everyone followed. Alfie filled his fork, putting the moist meat into his mouth.

Mrs Bodley caught his eye and raised her brows. She had been concerned that he would miss his father and had helped him make a card to send. He remembered what they'd added.

'Shall we fill it with a Christmas hug?' she had asked.

'Can we?'

He had put the card in the envelope. Before he'd closed it, she'd made him shut his eyes and remember the hug he'd given his father when he'd left Wyckerton. As Alfie had breathed out, she'd wafted the sigh into the envelope and quickly sealed it.

'There. When he opens this, he'll remember the hug, too,' she'd told him.

Like pixie dust, thought Alfie. He smiled back at her across the table to show that he felt fine.

'How are broom sales this year, Joshua?' asked Nigel.

'Very good. I've tried a new combination this year; balsawood stick with apple-blossom bristles. It's very light but not very strong. It's been a huge hit with young witches,' said Bun's father.

The enchanted table was the longest Alfie had seen it. It was covered in a thick white tablecloth. Three large bowls of sprawling greenery were equally spaced along the middle. Drinking glasses sparkled, reflecting the candles' flames. Silver crackers were placed by the plates. Each setting had had a napkin shaped like a witches hat. The feast was the best Alfie had ever tasted. His stomach felt so stretched he was sure he'd never be able to eat again.

Mrs Bodley put a huge plate on the table.

'Would anyone like a mince pie?' she said.

Alfie looked at the little pies. They were waddling down the centre of the table, ready to be picked up and eaten. Alfie shuddered. *I'll never be able to eat food that moves.*

Later, presents were passed from under another huge Christmas tree in the sitting room. Alfie opened the card and present from his father, sad that he wasn't with him.

Derek and Alfie ripped into their presents from each other and grinned as they both held up WarmDry gloves.

'We'll be able to have snowball fights for hours now,' said Derek.

Alfie watched as Mr and Mrs Bodley opened the present he'd bought them. The shopkeeper had assured him that the plain white boxes and packets in the wicker hamper would be everything they wanted. When Alfie had asked how it worked, the shopkeeper had explained that the hamper would suit the person it was given too, and magically become full of their favourite foods. His jaw dropped as they unwrapped it. He saw the brightly coloured boxes and packages instead of the plain white ones that he had wrapped.

Mrs Bodley smiled. 'Oh, everything we love. Thank you, Alfie.'

Alfie carefully unwrapped his present from them. A quill and a fountain pen.

'They're Spellright. One for home and one for school. They correct your spelling as you write.'

'Thank you.' Alfie always used a quill to write letters to his father and his homework but he had to write with a pen at school.

When Alfie was ready for bed, he left his new gloves next to Derek's on top of the dresser in the bedroom. They planned to get up early and play in the snow all day.

*

The snow had melted as Christmas became a memory. Alfie snuggled into the big, soft sofa in the sitting room. He watched as the frosts of the February evening took hold. He held one of the big books from the study, trying to find a clue. The muddle caused by breaking Mr Locksley's necklace had put him back at square one with a huge problem and no idea of how to solve it.

Ernie lay on the floor asleep. His ears pricked up. He raised his head as he heard something. Alfie looked up and listened. He could hear deep, male voices coming from the entrance hall. Ernie was content that he recognised them and moved towards the door to greet Mr Bodley as he walked into the room with Nigel.

'Brilliant game of golf. We really should play more often,' said Nigel.

Mr Bodley agreed. 'Now, are you sure you won't fetch Mary and come back for supper?'

'I would love to, but she's probably preparing our supper already. I need to eat quickly as I have to go to Alice's Apothecary Supplies to get more ingredients. It's been so busy I'm beginning to run low on a few items,' said Nigel. Realising that Alfie was there, he waved his hand towards him. 'How would you like to come along?'

'That would be brilliant! It'll be exciting to go somewhere new.' Alfie hadn't been to the suppliers before. This would be a chance to explore. 'Can Ernie come?'

Nigel nodded.

When Ernie heard his name he stood up again and waited.

'You'll have to wait a little while.' Alfie patted him on the head before turning back to look at Nigel. 'What time shall we meet you?'

'In about an hour, if that fits in?' Nigel looked at Mr Bodley who nodded.

'That should be fine. It smells like our supper's ready now,' said Mr Bodley, breathing in the aromas. He winked at Alfie. 'At least it won't be shepherd's pie!'

Nigel left. Alfie shut his book and returned it to the study. He grabbed the library chair and grinned as it unfolded and transformed into a pair of steps. He climbed up and returned the book to its place on the shelf just as the gong rang for suppertime.

*

Alfie arrived at Powerful Potions with Ernie just as Nigel came out of the door. He was carrying the bag that Alfie used for deliveries. This time it was full of empty, blue ingredient bottles.

Nigel didn't hurry as they strolled along the lanes, giving Alfie time to look around. A layer of frost covered the cobbles, managing to take hold even though they were being walked on. Doors and windows sparkled through their icy layer. Spider webs were clearly visible, easily supporting the weight of the ice crystals on them. He nuzzled into his cloak, glad he was wearing it.

As they walked away from the areas that Alfie knew, the streets became narrower. He looked down at the pavements. They were less tidy. Bits of rubbish blew around in the faint evening breeze. Ernie was fascinated by the smells and spent most of the time running behind them, sniffing the ground.

'Come on, Ernie, keep up or you'll have to go on your lead.' Alfie didn't want him dragging behind all the time.

The further they went from the city centre, the more crammed together the houses became. There were no front gardens. The only plants visible were in window boxes hanging from the first floor sills. Most were dead from the night frosts. The street lamps seemed dimmer. The weak, winter moonlight failed to get between the roofs to light the pathways.

Looking at the people as they walked past, Alfie could see that they weren't wealthy. Their clothes were a little less bright, as if they had been washed too many times. Though their friendly smiles made him feel safe.

'Even though this area's a little scruffy it feels safer than the Northeast Quarter, doesn't it?' said Alfie.

'Yes, everyone's friendly and likes to chat,' said Nigel. The journey had taken longer than it should, Nigel knew so many people that wanted to greet him.

Nigel stopped outside a little shop. 'This is it,' he said.

Alfie was surprised. He couldn't see through the glass.

'It's a bit grubby … and small,' he said, before he realised he was being rude.

Nigel walked to the door and opened it. He waggled it back and forth so that the bell rang excessively. Alfie winced at the harsh sound. His hands shot up to cover his ears. He was amazed that the door opened at all. It didn't look like it had been painted since it was new. The window was dirty; no lights visible inside. He would have sworn it was empty. Nigel ducked down to avoid hitting his head on the doorframe as he entered. Alfie peered through the open door before he followed.

He wasn't surprised that the inside was gloomy. Alfie recognised the aromatic smell. It was the same as Nigel's workshop. The counter was low and seemed to be made for a child-sized person. Drawers and cubbyholes lined the walls. Even though the ceiling was low, the amount of storage that was fitted neatly into the little room amazed Alfie. Row upon row of perfect square, wooden drawers with small glass eyeholes spread out before him. Most of the contents were visible through the glass and some of the colours that caught his eye were unique.

'It's like a doll's house-shop.' Alfie tried to explain what he was seeing.

'I know. Wait until you meet Alice,' whispered Nigel.

Since no one appeared, Nigel went back to the door and shook the bell with his hand.

'I'm coming, I'm coming. Patience is a virtue,' a croaky old voice sounded from the back room. A wizened old lady appeared at the door. If Alfie had ever been asked to describe a witch, it would have been her. All she needed was a wart on the end of her nose. She was tiny, cross, and very scary. Her long, thin hair was so white it was almost see-through and her little body was covered in a very old, well-worn gown. What Alfie found most strange was that her tiny feet were bare.

She came further into the room and squinted at Nigel.

'Oh, Nigel, it's you. How pleasant.' She smiled. She was smaller than Martha. Alfie saw the extraordinary colour of her eyes as they shone at him. They were a vivid orange with tawny specks that would have suited an eagle much more than they did a human.

'Good evening, Alice. This is my assistant, Alfie.'

Alfie smiled and nodded, still fascinated by her eyes.

'I'm in need of more ingredients,' said Nigel, and smiled fondly. 'I don't think I've ever been this busy.'

'You, too? Everyone seems to be running low on ingredients for potions at the moment,' she said, rubbing her tiny, pale hands together.

They continued chatting as Alfie tried to guess what was lurking behind the glass of some of the drawers. Nothing was labelled, but there were three or four hundred drawers. *How on earth can an old lady remember what she has here?* Nigel's ingredient bottles were clearly numbered and put in numerical order. It seemed strange that someone as fussy as Nigel would put his trust in a shop like this.

Nigel removed the blue bottles from the bag and started to list the ingredients he needed. At first they were familiar to Alfie. As Nigel continued, he asked for some things that Alfie hadn't heard of. Alice slowly made her way up and down a set of sliding steps collecting them together. She measured quantities on an antique pair of scales and placed them in Nigel's bottles on the old counter. Her crooked fingers looked like gnarled wands.

Eventually, Nigel said, 'Ground frogs spawn, green, not blue, please. And some dried dung-beetle spit?'

Alfie snorted, doubled up and headed for the door before he exploded.

'What's wrong with your friend?' enquired Alice croakily.

'I don't think he's heard of some of the ingredients we use.' Nigel ignored the fact that Alfie was struggling to open the door.

Alice put a couple of small spoonfuls of the green frogs spawn into a bottle.

'You won't use much,' she informed him. 'You do remember it's not for human consumption, don't you?'

'Yes, thank you.' Nigel smiled, not wanting to remind her that he was a very skilled potion maker.

Alfie was just about in control of himself by the time they left the shop. He was grateful that Derek wasn't there or they would still be laughing.

'I'm sorry, but *dried dung-beetle spit* sounded so funny,' he said.

'It's a very important ingredient,' said Nigel. He grinned, able to see how odd it sounded.

'Why do you shop there? She seemed a bit old to me. I'd be afraid that she'd forget what was in each drawer.'

'Her ingredients are the best you can buy. Those old drawers store things perfectly, which is the reason I always keep the minimum amount I can at my shop. Then everything is as fresh as possible.'

'But nothing is labelled. What if she gave you the wrong ingredient?' Alfie couldn't understand how she could remember every item.

'It's the way she works. When she inherited the shop, she had already worked there for most of her life. Knowing where her ingredients are stored is probably second nature to her.' Nigel didn't seem at all worried.

They continued to walk. Even though Alfie had been putting it off, he had to mention the smoke and vision he had seen with Derek in the workshop.

'Nigel, do you remember when Derek and I tidied the workshop on your anniversary?' he asked.

Nigel nodded.

'Well, something peculiar happened – ' Alfie was worried that Nigel would be cross.

Nigel looked at him and said, 'Sounds intriguing...'

Alfie glanced up at him to see if he looked annoyed. He didn't.

'We were tidying away all the ingredient bottles and the vials that you hadn't used. As we finished, we turned back towards the bench ...'

'Mm?' Nigel encouraged him to continue.

'I don't know what you left in the cauldron when you went out with Mary, but it made a white smoke and it billowed up, almost to the ceiling.'

Nigel raised his eyebrows.

'And a sort of vision appeared in it. We could see Mr Locksley, who was staying at the B&B, holding a necklace.'

'That seems odd,' said Nigel, frowning.

Alfie didn't continue. He didn't want tell him that the figure in the smoke turned into Nigel and that he had died.

'I don't think I left anything in the cauldron. I certainly hadn't been performing any ocular charms. I haven't had the need for ages.' Nigel seemed quite puzzled.

Alfie hadn't ever heard that word before. 'What's an ocla... ocu... that thing you said?'

'Ocular, it means visual. Sometimes they can help if I need to make a specific potion for someone.'

'How could it have happened then?' Alfie hoped that Nigel would have some answers.

'It's a bit of a mystery.' Nigel wrinkled his chin.

Alfie was disappointed that they were no closer to discovering the reason.

Nigel shook his head gently.

'I can't imagine why that happened, though...'

Alfie didn't want to interrupt Nigel's thoughts. He looked around. It had become busier. They were close to the city centre. He knew they'd be back at the B&B soon. He saw the old derelict house that he'd seen on a previous delivery. He hurried towards it so that he could have another look while Nigel caught up with him. He passed the rickety old building and stopped to look back. It looked even more impressive in the moonlight. Ernie sat down. Alfie looked up at the tall building, sad that such an elegant old structure was allowed to rot.

He felt the rumble deep inside him before he heard the cracking sound. He'd never heard anything like it. He raised his hands to protect his ears. The old building toppled over and slid across the road. The barricade was pushed along in a river of wood, bricks and plaster, followed by a mountain of white dust. The dust cloud tumbled towards him. His eyes closed automatically. He crouched down, covering his face and Ernie with his cloak. The air was too thick to breathe.

When the rumbling stopped and the ground felt stable again, he uncovered his eyes. Amazed, he glanced around at the mound of debris. If anything had been in its path, it would have been wiped out. He felt sick as he realised what had been in its path – *Nigel!* His chest hurt as he frantically scanned the area, fear rising in his throat. He ran towards the mound, unsure of what to do but needing to be closer. He caught sight of some cloaks moving at the leading edge of the debris. He tried to clamber towards them but his feet sank into the unstable rubble, preventing him from getting anywhere. He fell forward onto his hands and knees and started to crawl. As he moved closer he could see that two people were helping Nigel from the rubble. Nigel stood upright. He only looked dusty. The rubble had surrounded him rather than cover him.

Shocked, Alfie saw Richard holding his hands up as he magically held back the remains of the building. As everyone moved out of the way, he let the rubble fall into the space where Nigel had been.

Richard almost fell over as the effort took its toll. He sat down on the pile of debris and his head fell into his hands. His arms were too weak to support his head as he shook uncontrollably. Nigel smiled at Alfie, confirming that he was okay as he discussed the event with passers-by. Alfie ran to help Richard.

'You were amazing. Nigel's lucky you were here!' Alfie could see how exhausted Richard was. He looked as if he was made from wax – his cheeks were ghostly white. Alfie sat down beside him, afraid that the effort had been too much.

Bun appeared and said, 'What happened? I could feel the shudder in my house. Then I saw the cloud of dust.'

'That old building collapsed. Richard stopped it falling on Nigel,' answered Alfie.

'Good job you were here, Richard,' said Bun. He looked at him more closely. 'Are you alright?'

Richard didn't answer immediately. He tried to steady his breathing. 'I couldn't let him die.' The words hung in the air.

Alfie knew that Nigel would have been killed if Richard hadn't been there.

'Thank you,' whispered Alfie. 'We'll always remember this.'

*

Later, Derek and Chris listened in awe as Alfie and Bun told the story.

'Imagine what would have happened if Richard hadn't been there!' said Derek, shaking his head.

'I don't want to,' insisted Alfie, 'it would be too awful.' He couldn't bring himself to think of life without Nigel.

CHAPTER SEVENTEEN

Hydrolulous

THE cold weather became a distant memory as spring brought the plants to life. Trees had fresh, lime-green leaves on their branches. Around their trunks crocuses proudly showed their multi-coloured flower heads.

Alfie practised magic when he was alone. His control was really improving. Whenever he was out with Ernie, he would shut gates or tidy gardens without going anywhere near them.

He always tried to get his homework done on a Friday evening. This left the weekend totally free of schoolwork and avoided a panic on Sunday evening. He walked into the study to find Derek already sitting at the huge desk.

'I've almost finished my history. You can have the desk soon,' said Derek as he bent over his book.

'That's okay, I'll sit opposite you.' Alfie put his books down and pulled up a chair. He liked Derek to be around. They helped each other with some subjects. This way, neither sat there struggling. The thought of going into the city before bed helped him finish in record time. With his homework complete, Alfie shut his schoolbooks and smiled. The evening was now his to enjoy.

After supper he played in the city with Derek. The spring evening had a feeling of crispness. When he went to bed, the fresh outdoor smell had seeped into his clean sheets making him sleep soundly.

Alfie woke to the sound of bird song and wondered if they were happy because it was Saturday. He never noticed them on a weekday. He jumped out of bed and went into the bathroom before getting dressed.

'I can see that you're happy about going to Nigel's,' commented Mrs Bodley as he entered the kitchen.

Alfie could *feel* what she meant. Excitement always made his skin prickle on a Saturday. It was a whole day filled with magic. Being in the back of the shop making potions still fascinated him. Nigel included him at every stage. Alfie felt like an essential part of the team. Sometimes Nigel allowed him to make basic potions under supervision.

Alfie left the B&B after breakfast. The journey to Nigel's was second nature. He let his mind drift. At first, happy thoughts filled his head. Then worries started to creep in. By the time he arrived at the shop, he felt anxious.

Nigel was in his workshop. He looked up as Alfie entered.

'You look as though you've had a rough day already,' said Nigel. 'Are you okay?'

Alfie shrugged. He didn't want to tell Nigel that he was worried that Damian was still trying to kill him. Time was running out. The necklace hadn't helped. Nigel hadn't believed him before but he knew the threat was still there – he didn't have any new information, just an uncomfortable feeling.

Alfie didn't know how to explain his glum expression. He said the first thing that popped into his head. 'School exams are getting closer. I don't expect I'll do very well.'

'As long as you try your best. No one expects any more than that,' said Nigel.

Alfie was pleased that he'd fooled Nigel and not let on about Damian. Then he wondered how he could convince his teachers that he'd tried his best.

'I think I do,' he said.

'So – try a little bit harder, until you *know* you do!' Nigel smiled at him.

Alfie screwed up his nose.

'Ha!' said Nigel. 'You know you're not trying hard enough, then?'

Alfie guessed he could spend less time worrying about Nigel and more time on his schoolwork.

'Anyway, I know you try your best when you're here. Let's make these potions, shall we?' Nigel changed the subject.

Alfie breathed a sigh of relief as they settled into their usual routine. Nigel explained what he was adding and told Alfie what he would need next, so that he had it ready at the right time. Some of the potions started off very similar but the last few ingredients that went in, or the way they were added, made them very different.

'Do you know everything about potion making?'

'I don't think anyone does. New ingredients are being discovered all the time. Things that I would never have thought of using,' said Nigel.

'Like what?'

'I always used plain dried lizard's liver, until a witch named Ilsa discovered that if it's soaked with ginger root in olive oil, and re-dried, it's much more potent.'

The variations seemed endless to Alfie.

They stopped for lunch. Then he looked after the shop for Mary while she went to the hairdresser's for a couple of hours. Alfie enjoyed serving the non-magics and listening to them discuss Wyckerton. The tourists talked about discovering the old parts of the city or how much the guided tours had taught them.

Most of all he enjoyed listening to the local people from the surrounding villages. They would chat as if Wyckerton was theirs. He smiled. They thought it was an ordinary city.

When Mary returned, Alfie and Nigel went to the workshop and finished making the rest of the potions for delivery.

'How's the magic coming along?' asked Nigel.

'Brilliantly! I practise a lot.' Alfie grinned.

'That's good. Perhaps today we could try something a little harder.' Nigel raised his eyebrows.

'The harder the better!' said Alfie, accepting the challenge.

Nigel moved so that the space around him was clear.

'The stance is similar to the spells I've shown you before. Balance in the centre, knees relaxed. You might find that you develop your own way of standing eventually.' He looked at Alfie who was copying his movements. 'I thought we could try the liquid charm.'

Alfie giggled and imagined water rising up out of a pot like a snake and slowly waving from side to side.

'When you're ready.' Nigel waited patiently.

Alfie stopped grinning. 'Sorry.'

'Your hand movements reflect what you want the water to do. If you want it to rise up, you act as if your hand is underneath.' Nigel's hand was palm up. He lowered his arm so that it looked like he was going to scoop something up. 'You raise your arm with your hand fully open, as if you're lifting the water.'

Alfie copied the movements.

'Good. If you wanted to hold the water back, you would swing your arm in from the side and raise your hand with your palm facing the water, *forbidding* it to come towards you.'

Alfie copied him again.

Nigel nodded. 'Well done. Now you can try to do it using this water.' Nigel went over to the bench to fetch a full water jug. Alfie thought that he would be making it move in the jug but Nigel poured it onto the floor, creating a puddle. 'As you do the movement, you say *Hydrolulous…*'

Alfie repeated the word a few times. When Nigel nodded, he moved towards the water. He decided to get it to rise up first. He relaxed his body and found his balance.

He scooped his hand, raising his palm upwards, and said, *'Hydrolulous!'*

The water rippled as if it had been blown by a gentle breeze. It made tiny waves but didn't rise up like a snake. Alfie lowered his hand and tried again. The waves were still small but slightly more defined.

'Not bad,' said Nigel.

Alfie frowned at him, disappointed in himself.

'Water is notoriously difficult,' explained Nigel.

Alfie snorted and moved his feet to see if that would help.

'Hydrolulous!' The movement and word came together. The water

reacted. All the ripples joined together. The water rose as if it were being drawn up through a thick straw.

'Yes!' Alfie pulled his fist towards his chest in victory. He jumped out of the way as the water dived towards his feet. He was too late.

Nigel's laughter hooted out.

'You were still controlling it!'

Alfie looked at his wet shoes and socks. They were both laughing as they heard the city bell toll.

'Ah, the sound of freedom.' Nigel smiled.

Alfie grinned back, understanding what he meant.

They heard the door chime ring. Alfie went through to the shop knowing that Mary would have left for the day. He watched as Richard came in. He looked awful. His skin was even paler than the first time he had come into the shop. The dark rings under his eyes looked like they'd been painted with a black brush. He didn't approach the counter but headed straight for the chair and sat down.

Nigel came through from the back.

'Richard, how are you?'

'I've been better,' Richard responded slowly.

Alfie could see that he was suffering. The effort of coming here had obviously taken its toll on his energy.

'Have a rest. Can I get you a drink?' Alfie wanted him to be comfortable after what he'd done to save Nigel.

'Thank you, but no,' said Richard. He looked at Nigel. 'I was wondering if you could make me some more painkillers, perhaps a little stronger this time?' He grimaced, as if he couldn't stand the pain.

'Of course, I'll do it right now.' Nigel disappeared towards the workshop.

'How is your quest going?' asked Richard.

'Not well. We have to find it soon.'

'*It.* What do you mean? I thought you said *someone* was trying to harm Nigel.' Richard seemed interested despite his discomfort.

Alfie looked into Richard's eyes. The whites were yellow as if his body was finding it hard to cope with his prolonged pain.

'They are but they need an object to help,' said Alfie. 'I'm determined to find it first!'

Richard nodded. 'And that object was supposed to be that necklace?'

Alfie nodded. He wanted to ask him if he thought Damian could be the culprit but he knew Nigel would tell him off for accusing Damian without proof.

'Don't give up. That's my motto. Something will turn up to help. Keep on looking,' Richard tried to sound encouraging.

Nigel had worked at lightning speed and came back carrying the bottle of medication. 'This should do the trick.' He'd also brought a dropper so that Richard could take some before he left. 'Why don't you stay and have a cup of tea with me. Alfie was just about to do his deliveries.'

'That would make me feel better,' said Richard.

Alfie went to the workshop and collected the potions that they had prepared earlier. He carefully placed them in the pockets of the bag. He set off on his rounds, pleased that he was getting to know his way around the streets of Wyckerton.

CHAPTER EIGHTEEN

The Challenge

THE fresh lime-green leaves of spring were turning darker as summer approached. Alfie's schoolteachers praised him for being more confident. He didn't try to be invisible during class discussions. He found joining in easier. He almost enjoyed school.

Alfie half-listened during his third lesson. Mrs Stott asked them to find facts about the Jurassic coast. 'Silently!' She added.

Alfie thought silently meant permission to daydream. *I hate geography.* He felt his vision blur. As his mind drifted, the ordinary surroundings disappeared and magic influenced his imagination. The shuffling around him brought his attention back to the classroom. Mrs Stott was out of her seat and moving around her desk towards the pupils.

'I need a couple of volunteers…' droned Mrs Stott, getting closer to Alfie and Derek. Derek tried to shrink away.

Alfie looked at Bun in desperation. *Do something!* he mouthed, needing Bun's charm to fool Mrs Stott.

Bun looked around the room. 'Have you finished your maths homework, Eric?' he called out.

Eric looked at him and frowned. 'Of course I have. I always do my homework as soon as it's set.' He glanced at Mrs Stott, hoping for praise.

Mrs Stott swung around in Eric's direction. 'Then you'll have the time to help me during break!' she said. 'And you, too,' she nodded towards the boy seated next to Eric. 'For starters, the blackboard needs a proper clean and the dusters are disgusting!'

Eric scowled at Bun. He seemed unsure of how Bun had made it happen, but he mouthed, *I'll get you back for this!*

Bun winked at him.

When Bun looked at Alfie, he signalled with thumbs up. Alfie shook his head. How did Bun think that up so quickly? He seemed to know how Eric and Mrs Stott would react. The end of lesson bell vibrated and everyone stood up.

'SIT DOWN!' Mrs Stott instructed loudly. 'The bell is for *my* benefit, *not* yours. Right, you can finish what you were doing for your homework,' she stated.

Dregs – homework, Alfie thought, regretting that he had not concentrated earlier.

'You may all leave after me!' she bellowed. She turned back to Eric and said, 'I'll be back shortly.'

They were the last to leave the room and just as they were about to go through the door, Eric called out, 'Organise a game of Manhunt tonight, Bun. If I'm *It*, I'm coming after you first!'

'The game decides who's *It*. Shall we say eight o'clock?' said Bun, accepting the challenge.

Eric nodded, his smile lopsided.

Alfie took a deep breath. His nerves jangled. *Blimey! My first game of Manhunt!* He couldn't wait to race through the city on broomsticks.

They went outside and stood in the queue for the tuck shop. Jazz and Martha were ahead of them.

Chris went up and spoke to them. As he came back he said, 'That's sorted. They're going to let everyone know about Manhunt tonight.'

Alfie's stomach fizzed. As his smile faded, he remembered his last magic lesson. 'Nigel showed me something new on Saturday. It was pretty difficult. We only used a jug full of water.'

His friends laughed. Alfie realised how silly it had sounded but he had to be careful about what he said in front of non-magics.

'I heard you shouting in the bathroom while you practised. I guessed what it was,' said Derek.

'Something to do with water, then?' asked Bun.

Alfie nodded.

'Really difficult. None of us are that good,' said Derek.

After school, they walked home. As usual, they separated at the end of Bun's street.

'Meet you at the park at eight o'clock,' Alfie reminded them as they walked away. He wasn't sure he could wait that long.

When the supper gong sounded, Alfie and Derek were the first to arrive in the kitchen. They waited eagerly as the others drifted in. As soon as Aunt Edith lifted a spoon to serve herself, they dived in and filled their plates.

'*What* is wrong with you two?' asked Mrs Bodley. 'You're going to give yourselves indigestion. Slow down!'

Neither of them answered. Their mouths were jammed full of food.

She glared at them. 'If you can't eat properly, you'll have to miss supper and go to your room!'

They both swallowed.

'Sorry!' they said in unison.

Alfie behaved perfectly for the rest of the meal. He wasn't going to mess up his first game of Manhunt.

'We've had a letter inviting us to the parents' meetings next month. Your father has asked us to take responsibility for you, Alfie,' said Mrs Bodley.

'When is it?' asked Derek.

'The third Saturday of the month. In the afternoon,' responded Mrs Bodley.

'Why is it on a Saturday? That's stupid,' announced Alfie.

'It would hardly be in the evening, would it?' said Mr Bodley. 'Only some of the parents and teachers would turn up!' He laughed aloud.

'We don't have to come, do we? I help Nigel on Saturdays. I don't want to miss that,' asked Alfie.

'No. The teachers will probably prefer it with fewer children at the school,' said Mrs Bodley.

Relieved, Alfie leant back in his chair and finished his meal before they left with their broomsticks and ran towards the park.

CHAPTER NINETEEN

Manhunt

'I never thought we were going to get out of there in time!' puffed Derek as they raced along the streets.

Alfie was silent.

'What's up?' asked Derek.

'Are the rules exactly like Manhunt at school?'

'Almost. One person starts as *It*, or the predator. They have to catch prey. That's everyone else, until there's only the winner left. There's help from miniature stone statues, called effigies, scattered around the city that do different things. They aid the predators at first but when the number of people on each side becomes equal, they change loyalty to the prey,' explained Derek.

'How do they work?'

'When they're grabbed and thrown, they become the live version of whatever they're an effigy of. They slow down your enemy or hide your movements so that you can change direction without being seen. There are six types. With several of each type to be spread all over the city. There's a rope net. That's thrown at an opponent. If you get caught in the net, it's harder to fly. There's a flock of birds. They grab the enemy's broom and pull them backwards, which slows them down.'

'That sounds horrid. Do they attack you?' asked Alfie.

'No. They just go for the broom.'

Alfie puffed out, relieved.

'If you think the birds are horrid, wait until you see the cloud of bats. They fly straight at you to put you off,' Derek shuddered. 'That's probably my least favourite. Umm… there's a smoke screen. Obviously, when that effigy's thrown it makes a huge cloud of white smoke.'

'Why would that affect anyone? You'd just fly through it.'

'Yes, but you can change direction quickly, while your enemy can't see you.'

Alfie nodded. 'Nice tactics!'

'Thanks!' said Derek. 'There's also a compass.'

Alfie wasn't impressed. 'So … North, East, South, West. How does that help?'

Derek laughed.

'It points to the nearest opponent. It could lead a predator to prey. It could also show prey where the nearest predator is, so that they don't fly towards them.'

'That is impressive!' admitted Alfie.

'Lastly is the Newton. It adds a lead weight to the broom tip which makes it dive toward the ground.'

Alfie frowned. 'Don't people get hurt?'

'No. It detaches before they hit the ground. Basically, they all give a few seconds to catch someone or aid escape.'

Alfie thought it sounded awesome. He couldn't wait. He started to run. A small crowd of children had already gathered in the park. Alfie didn't know everyone there. He guessed the oldest was about sixteen. He was holding a small, velvet bag.

Bun and Chris came over to them.

'I'm relying on you three to watch my back,' said Bun.

'We owe you one for saving us from Mrs Stott,' said Alfie.

'If I get caught before you, I'll give you one chance to escape, then we're equal,' said Derek.

'Watch it or next time I'll let Stotty have you!' said Bun.

Alfie looked from one to the other. He could feel the tension that the looming game created.

'We shouldn't get caught too quickly with Alfie around,' said Chris, looking at Alfie.

Alfie thought he was taking the mickey. 'Why?'

'You must know the streets pretty well by now with all those potion deliveries.'

'Good point. Alfie, we'll rely on you to keep us one step ahead,' said Bun.

Alfie wasn't sure that was a good idea. He knew the streets when he was walking, but from the air they would look totally different.

The oldest boy shouted, 'If you're ready, I'm opening the bag!'

Excitement echoed around the park as everyone formed a circle and mounted their brooms. The older boy walked into the middle and put the velvet bag on the floor. The bag was moving, as if a cat was trying to escape.

Alfie stared. 'What's in the bag?'

'All of the live versions of the effigies,' said Derek. 'They come out of the bag as the live things: nets, birds, bats and the rest. They go and hide around the city and that's when they turn to stone. When they're grabbed and used, they become real again.'

The older boy took a huge step away from the bag and reached out. His hand shook as he carefully untied the red ribbon that held the bag shut. He jumped away, running to join the circle. The ribbon slid to the ground. Alfie held his breath. Silence hung in the air as if the bag was a black hole and all sound had been sucked into it.

A faint fluttering was the only warning. The bag erupted, smoke shot high into the air. It swirled around, growing bigger. Birds and bats spewed out, along with several rope nets. Metal compasses and lead weights quickly followed. The bag belched out another cloud of smoke that slowly rose up. Everything spiralled above them like a tornado. Alfie couldn't take his eyes off the swirling mass. He almost left his skin behind as he jumped at the loud cracking sound the tornado made as it broke up and scattered throughout the city.

'Remember, at the beginning of the game they're on the predator's side. Any effigies you find will have a red tinge. They can only be used by predators. When half the prey have been caught, they change sides and have a blue tinge,' explained Derek.

Alfie hoped that he would get to use a blue effigy and wasn't caught immediately.

'I forgot to mention the ribbons,' said Derek. 'The red one that tied the bag will decide who is the first predator by tying itself on to the tip of their broom. It divides and tethers onto the broom of any prey that's caught, showing that they've become predators.

When there's only one prey left, a gold ribbon will appear on their broom tip, showing that they're the winner.'

The red ribbon rose up and hovered before it moved slowly around the circle.

'When someone is chosen, fly away as quickly as possible,' whispered Derek.

The ribbon stopped in front of Alfie. He held his breath.

'Unless it chooses you, of course!' said Chris, inching away.

The ribbon moved on slowly. Eric waggled his broom tip trying to get in the ribbon's way. He was grinning at Bun. Alfie was relieved to see that it was friendly rivalry. Eric looked disappointed as it moved past. Suddenly it struck a broom, wrapping itself around the tip and flapping wildly.

'SCATTER!' someone shouted. The circle disappeared into the sky.

Alfie yanked his broomstick and flew straight up. He was stunned that Derek, Bun and Chris found him in the chaos. They were all flying faster than he'd ever thought possible.

'We stick together as long as we can,' shouted Derek.

The difference in flying was unbelievable. The thought of being hunted made him feel even more capable.

'We need to find a better position,' said Bun. 'Any ideas, Alfie?'

Alfie looked around to get his bearings.

'The streets get really narrow over there,' he pointed towards some alleyways. 'They wind and turn for ages.'

Bun headed off and they followed. They dived down and clung to the buildings. The narrow streets intensified their speed. There was hardly time to think.

Alfie's heart was pounding. He felt scared and excited. The walls of buildings rushed past. He couldn't focus on anything. He was passing at lightning speed.

He heard a noise behind him and looked back. Two girls were following them. He tried to see the tip of their brooms.

'I can't see a ribbon,' shouted Alfie.

'Neither can I. They're probably trying to keep out of the way, too,' replied Chris.

Alfie watched as the two girls slowed down and hid between two buildings.

Alfie directed the others along a tiny alley. It was almost a walkway. The spikes of Derek's broom bristles ahead of him threatened to poke his eyes out if they stopped quickly. He eased back slightly and shook his head in awe. The alley was so narrow it seemed as if they were flying up a chimney, their broom bristles almost cleaned the sides as they whizzed along. They slowed down and flew towards the gutter of the roof and hovered.

Bun was about to move off.

Alfie heard a scraping sound. 'Watch out!' he shouted.

Three boys shot out of an alleyway. Two girls followed them. One girl threw an effigy. It immediately became a net and wrapped around one of the boys. He struggled against it, giving the girl time to catch up. The other girl was faster and better on her broom than the remaining boys. She caught one easily. Alfie watched as new ribbons peeled off from the girls' brooms and tied themselves around the tips of the boys' brooms.

'Dregs,' said Derek. 'Two more predators to watch out for.'

The group of four predators set off after the third boy.

'That was close!' said Bun. 'Don't know how you saw them. I wouldn't have.'

'Yeah, nicely spotted, Alfie,' said Chris.

Alfie blew out his cheeks and laughed. He was torn between fear and excitement.

They hovered silently in the shadows watching as predators chased prey above them. They slowly edged out of cover. They crept up the building's roof toward the ridge so that they had a wider view.

The moonlit sky was alive with witches and wizards on broomsticks. Small and large groups were whizzing around, making use of safety in numbers. Lone prey desperately looked for places to hide. One predator threw an effigy, which turned into a net and tangled around a rider. Another skilfully threw one in front of a prey and caught them as they swerved to avoid the bats. One chased a prey. He was alone and had no effigies. He relied purely on speed.

Alfie gasped, feeling stupid. The scene was the same as it had been from his old bedroom window. These were the odd-looking birds he had watched.

His hands slipped and the broom wobbled as out of nowhere two predators whizzed past. They screeched to a halt and turned back, hovering.

Alfie couldn't help ducking even though he was sure he was hidden behind the ridge. He saw a red-tinged, mini-effigy. He watched as one of the predators grabbed it and it became real.

'Oh no! They have a compass. It'll point straight at us,' whispered Alfie. He gripped his broomstick, ready to fly.

'Shh,' whispered Bun, 'wait for my signal. We might not be the closest prey to them.'

They continued to hover quietly. Alfie's instinct was telling him to run but he trusted the others. He spotted the silhouette of a lone prey behind a crooked chimney. The two predators followed the guide of the compass and sped towards it, red ribbons flapping. The solitary prey shot out from behind the chimney and towards the moon. Alfie recognised who it was from his size.

'That prey was Eric. If he gets caught, you'll be first on his list,' said Alfie, looking across at Bun.

'Doesn't mean he'll catch me,' said Bun.

'We ought to move. He might have spotted where we were hiding. He'll head straight back here,' said Derek.

The others waited for instruction. Alfie pointed towards some buildings and indicated downwards. They moved off again, slowly at first. They used the buildings as cover and picked up speed when it was clear.

Alfie dipped his head to wipe his sweaty forehead on his sleeve, not daring to take his hand off the broomstick. His knowledge of the city's narrow alleyways impressed the others. They moved along street after street, trying to remain hidden. They turned up a narrower lane when Bun swerved to grab something. Alfie realised it was an effigy. The stone had lost its red tint. Now it was blue.

'They've change sides,' said Derek. 'More than half of us have been caught!' he reminded Alfie.

They gained some height. The mass of players became visible again. The huge number of flapping red ribbons was threatening.

'Odds are against us. Look at all those red ribbons,' said Bun. 'What do you think we should do, Derek?'

Alfie was pleased that Derek was there. He was the best at weighing up the risks.

'I think we should make a dash for the edge of the Northeast Quarter. At least half of the predators will be too scared to look there. Which way, Alfie?' asked Derek.

Alfie looked out at the battle.

'Cover will be limited from here. Maybe we should go as quickly as we can through the battle.' Alfie's mouth felt dry at the thought.

They all looked out towards the mayhem.

'Let's just do it!' exclaimed Chris.

'Okay, but if we manage to get there, we don't want to go into the Northeast Quarter. No one really knows what happens there, especially at night,' said Derek, refusing to move until they all agreed.

They set off and skimmed across the rooftops, picking up speed. They were desperate to get through the chaos as quickly as possible. They dodged around smaller chases, excited by being so close. Chris used his bulk to clear a path. Alfie noticed and pulled in behind him, followed by the other two.

Alfie sensed they were being followed. When he looked back he saw Eric chasing them. Alfie's broomstick wobbled as he shouted, 'It's Eric!'

'This is it!' shouted Bun. 'Get behind me until I give the word, then move aside. I'll hit him with this.' He waved the effigy.

They did as he ordered. Alfie looked back. Eric was gaining on them. Alfie felt like a rabbit being chased by a fox. Eric was so close. Alfie looked back and down as Eric's outstretched hand reached for his ankle. Alfie's heart missed a beat.

'NOW!' shouted Bun.

Alfie swerved away from Eric as Derek and Chris separated, too. Bun threw the effigy, which grew and turned into a lead weight, like the ones chained to ankles of prisoners.

'NEWTON!' shouted Bun, triumphantly.

It happened exactly like Derek had explained. The lead weight hit Eric and its chain instantly attached to his broom tip. He plunged towards the ground. Alfie sighed with relief.

'I think that's the best effigy,' said Bun, laughing.

They flew on towards the Northeast Quarter. Alfie noticed blue effigies hovering in various places. There didn't seem to be a pattern to where they were. He moved towards one and grabbed it. A flock of tiny birds were carved out of stone.

'I have a bird one!' he shouted to the others.

He looked behind, hoping to see a predator. One was chasing them. He threw the effigy, not waiting for the predator to catch up. As it left his hand, it grew into a flock of birds, much larger than the effigy. They swooped around the predator and grabbed the bristles of his broom. They beat their wings wildly against his forward motion and slowed him down.

'Well done, good shot!' shouted Chris.

'You should wait until predators are closer. You'd have missed with the other things. Only the birds and bats will hit predators from that distance,' advised Derek.

Alfie still felt triumphant. The next effigy he threw exploded into a mass of bats. They flew straight at the predators, diving away at the last second before returning again and again. The predators all raised an arm to cover their faces in defence. They wobbled on their broomsticks and slowed down. Alfie cringed – he wouldn't be able to cope with creepy bats either.

He grabbed another effigy, which turned into a compass. It took a few seconds to get its bearings. Then the needle started to circle around wildly. He frowned as he held it out so that Derek could see.

Derek seemed edgy. 'That means we're surrounded.'

Alfie looked around and saw predators moving in from all

directions. He frantically tried to see a way out.

He spotted another effigy. 'Quickly, Chris, there's an effigy just below you!' he shouted.

Chris swung his broom around and dived towards it. He grabbed it.

'When I throw this, head straight up!' he screamed, his voice cracked under the pressure.

The predators moved closer.

'NOW!' shouted Chris, throwing the effigy.

Alfie pulled hard and shot straight upward. He looked down and saw a sheet of white smoke.

Derek joined him. 'That was a smoke-screen,' he said.

'Where are Bun and Chris? Should we wait?' asked Alfie.

It seemed hard for Derek to make the decision. His loyalty made him hesitate. They both stared at the white smoke, waiting.

Suddenly, Bun and Chris flew out of the smoke with all the predators. Red ribbons on the tips of their brooms.

'NO!' shouted Derek. His decision came too late.

They frantically flew away but the group of predators pursuing them was huge. Almost everyone had been caught.

'Separate,' shouted Derek. 'Good luck.' He swerved away to the left with half the pack close on his tail.

The rest closed in on Alfie. He slipped his hands along his broomstick so that his body lay flat. He was sure he could smell birds and bats on his hands from the effigies even though they were carved from stone. His eyes started to water as he blinked rapidly against the wind. He tried to shield them behind his sleeves. He didn't get far before he felt a hand on his shoulder. The red ribbon peeled off his captor's broom tip and wrapped itself around the tip of his. He slowed down and watched Derek approach with a ribbon already attached to his broom.

'Who won?' asked Derek. 'I thought we were the last to be caught.'

A silhouette appeared in the distance. The gold ribbon on its broom tip glowed in the moonlight.

It was Martha.

'I won, I actually won!' she said, elated. Her grin stretched from ear to ear.

'Well done!' said several players in unison.

'Game over,' said the oldest boy.

Effigies filled the sky as they became live and zoomed off towards the park. The players followed. Martha was in front.

Everyone spoke at the same time.

'Well done!'

'Brilliant game.'

'That was the longest I've ever played before I was caught.'

'What a game! Did you see me throw that smokescreen?'

'Well done, Martha.'

Alfie watched as Eric flew up behind Bun.

'Caught you eventually!' Eric slapped Bun on the back, making him wobble.

'Took you long enough,' responded Bun, joking.

They arrived at the park as everything flew back into the bag. One by one the ribbons untied from the broom tips, united into one and floated to seal the bag.

Martha smiled proudly. 'I can't wait until the next game.'

'Nor can I,' said Alfie, his face ached as he gave her an exhausted grin.

*

Alfie and Derek discussed the game as they walked home. Alfie's arms waved around as he explained a really good manoeuvre that he'd made. He jumped as his shoulder rammed into someone walking on the pavement.

'I'm sorry,' said Alfie before he recognised the man. 'Oh hello, Richard.' Alfie was pleased to see that he was looking much better. Nigel's potion was obviously helping.

'Hello, I didn't know you lived around here.' Richard smiled.

'Yes, at Park Your Broomstick. I hope you didn't have to visit Nigel for more painkillers?'

'No, just visiting someone else,' he said and nodded his farewell.

They arrived back at the B&B. As they went through the front door, Mrs Bodley was walking through the entrance hall on the way to the kitchen.

'Ah, that was good timing. A letter has just arrived for you, Alfie. It's on the tray.' Mrs Bodley's head-nod indicated the letter tray that was kept on the sideboard.

'Thank you,' said Alfie and picked up the envelope.

Derek put the brooms in the broom cupboard and ran up the stairs.

Alfie looked at the beautiful writing. It almost danced across the space. Delicate letters flowed together to make up the words. He didn't know anyone who wrote like that. He carefully tore the seal to get to the contents, slid out a card and read:

If you have a task but dwindling will…

Alfie's hands shook as he finished reading and the card fluttered to the floor. He bent down, scooped it up and ran to the sitting room. As he entered, he shouted Derek's name but only heard a murmur from Aunt Edith as she stirred.

'Sorry!' he shouted as he turned. 'Didn't mean to disturb you.' He left the room and headed towards the staircase. Nearing the top of the second set, he wished that their room were closer even though he usually loved the privacy it gave him. The brick staircase was the hardest to climb in a hurry because it was narrow and solid. He stopped outside the bedroom to catch his breath, before he turned the handle.

Derek was sitting on his bed. He seemed to sense the urgency that oozed from Alfie.

'Are you okay?' He almost finished the words before Alfie was fully in the room.

'No. Look at this…' He handed Derek the card.

If you have a task but dwindling will,
Use the wishing well to fulfil.

'What does it mean?' asked Derek.

'I think it means that we could make a wish to find the object that Damian needs to kill Nigel.' He looked at the envelope again and frowned in confusion. He showed Derek. 'Look, it isn't even addressed to me.' Derek's shoulders rose, confused. 'Mrs Bodley said a letter had arrived for me, but my name's not on it.'

Alfie was sure he'd seen his name on the envelope, too. Could they both have been wrong? He turned and made his way back down the stairs. Derek jumped up and followed him.

They entered the kitchen and Alfie said, 'Why did you think that letter was for me?'

Mrs Bodley's voice broke with a single note of laughter. 'Because it was addressed to you.' She looked at him as if he'd gone mad.

'But it wasn't. Look.' He held out the envelope.

'Oh.' She looked confused. 'Maybe I just assumed it was because I didn't recognise the writing.'

Alfie showed her the card.

'It's probably just to get the tourists to go to that part of town,' she said.

As they left the kitchen Alfie said, 'I think we need to go to this wishing well. Where is it?'

'I've never heard anyone talk about it,' said Derek as he shrugged.

Alfie turned the card over. 'Ah, there's a map!'

Derek moved closer.

'It's in the Northeast Quarter.' Derek swallowed and looked at Alfie before looking at the map again. He sighed with relief. 'But not in too far.'

'That doesn't matter. We'll go during the day so that we'll be safe.' Alfie was pleased that he sounded so confident. 'We can take Ernie,' he added, before he realised that taking a huge German Shepherd dog might prove that he was also scared.

CHAPTER TWENTY

The Wishing Well

ALFIE and Derek decided to go to the wishing well before school the next day. They went down to the kitchen early. Some guests were already having breakfast and the regulars chatted to the more recent arrivals. Alfie wondered how many people the enchanted table could actually seat.

'Try the Bananaberries, Alfie,' said Mrs Bodley.

He reluctantly took one but was pleasantly surprised by the juicy sweetness. The taste of banana lingered as he looked around. He felt as though he belonged among wizards. His broom flying was excellent and his magical skills were developing nicely. He knew his friends had noticed.

'Have any of you been to the wishing well?' he asked.

'In Wyckerton?' responded Aunt Edith.

'Yes. Have you?' said Alfie. He hadn't considered that she would have gone there. It was a long way to walk.

'I didn't even know there was one. It's not the sort of thing I would expect to find in this city,' said Aunt Edith as she shook her head gently.

'It's probably just for tourists. I think non-magics like that sort of thing,' said Mr Bodley.

Alfie worried that the wishing well wouldn't help but he had to try everything.

'Why do you ask?' asked Mrs Bodley.

Alfie muttered, 'I was just thinking about the letter that arrived yesterday and wondered if any of you believed in the power of wishing wells.'

'I wouldn't write off anything. Nobody really knows,' said Mrs Bodley.

'No.' Alfie thought back to last summer. 'Not everyone believes in magic, you know!'

Everyone laughed.

Alfie and Derek decided against taking Ernie. They left soon after breakfast. Alfie ignored the little seed of doubt that kept popping into his head. This *had* to work. They walked along the wide, pleasant main street and passed the market square. They reached the narrow streets quickly. Alfie's quickened pulse warned him that he'd entered the Northeast Quarter. He felt uneasy; his insides squirmed as if they wanted to hide. His hearing felt sharp and smells gathered around his nostrils, warning him that it was an unpleasant place. He finally understood what *fight or flight* meant. He was ready to run if he had to. He glanced at Derek and could tell he felt the same.

Derek had the map and led them along some narrow streets that criss-crossed each other until he stopped at a blockade. The attached sign said: *Essential maintenance for twenty-four hours, ending at midnight. The Highways and Byways Agency apologise for any inconvenience.*

'This is the way in…' said Derek. He continued to stand looking at the sign.

'Dregs!' said Alfie with feeling. 'Today of all days. Is this the only route?'

'It looks like it,' Derek held up the map so that Alfie could see, 'it leads into a big square with the old well in the middle. We could try and find another entrance.'

Alfie shook his head. 'No, we could get really lost. Then we'd be late for school.' He thought for a moment. 'We'll get Bun and Chris to come back with us.' He read the sign again. 'Sometime after midnight when the barrier's gone.'

Derek didn't look pleased.

His voice cracked, 'It will be completely dark by then.'

'I know, I'm fed up with wasting time. I don't want to wait until tomorrow.' Alfie didn't want to let Nigel down. 'Come on. Let's warn the others of what we've lined up for them later.'

They retraced their steps until they were almost back at the city centre.

'Let's go around to Bun's house. Catch him before school,' said Derek as they neared the end of Bun's street.

Alfie had never been to Bun's home. He liked the friendly row of Victorian terraced houses set back behind a wall. Small iron gates led to a path and a front door. Derek knocked at the only blue door. Bun's mother answered and called him.

Bun smiled when he saw them. When he noticed how serious they looked, he moved into the front garden before asking what they wanted.

Alfie explained about the wishing well, '... we thought we'd meet and go later tonight, after the barrier has gone,' he finished.

Bun nodded. 'Okay. Chris will be along in a minute. We can tell him on the way to school. If we meet here at midnight, it should be gone by the time we get there.'

'I'm taking my broomstick just in case I need it!' Derek informed them.

'Good idea,' said Bun.

Alfie wondered what use the brooms would be as they walked to the corner to meet Chris. They rounded the corner at the end of Bun's road and waited as Chris approached. Alfie recognised the semi-cleared area where the old derelict house had stood. *That explains how Bun arrived so quickly when it collapsed. His garden must back on to it.*

*

It was almost midnight as they walked towards Bun's house. He was already waiting outside. As they moved closer, Chris jumped out at them.

Derek swore.

Alfie's hand shot up to cover his heart.

'What the ...' Alfie wasn't pleased. 'Bun's Mum will hear us!' He tried to keep his voice as quiet as possible.

'Sorry … didn't think of that,' said Chris.

Alfie snorted.

'Just keep quiet,' said Derek.

The initial streets on their journey were well lit. The chatting and laughing of the last few adults leaving a café peeled through the air, amplified by the surrounding sleepy silence. They turned into a side street and headed north, leaving familiar sounds behind.

Derek's idea to take the broomsticks had been a good one. Alfie felt safer just carrying his. He couldn't imagine when they would use them. The streets were far too narrow. Alfie saw the entrance looming ahead. He was pleased that the sign had been removed. They walked along the pathway and left their brooms at the entrance to the square.

Alfie was disappointed when he saw the well. The wall surrounding it was low, making it look very ordinary. He took a deep breath to reassure himself that it would work and made his way over to it, followed by the others. The four of them stood and looked into the hole.

Alfie reached into his pocket and brought out a coin.

'I'm going to drop this in and wish.' He closed his eyes and moved his hand over the cavernous hole. He wished to find the object and dropped the coin.

The silence seemed to go on forever. Then they heard a tiny plop as it hit the water.

'Now we just have to wait and see if …' Alfie's voice broke off as a thunderous sound came up from the depths of the well. They all realised at the same time that something alarming was happening below. They started to run towards the exit where the barrier had been.

Alfie didn't want to look back towards the well but he couldn't help it. His heart pounded in his chest. Fear closed his throat. The amount of water rising up from the mouth of the well was vast. As it left the funnel, it spread out like a carpet of liquid grey steel.

It turned towards them – a sea of white, angry horses. Their heads were lowered and their mouths open, ready to attack. Alfie's legs felt light, like the wind, as he ran. Fear made him stop. His friends were in danger because of him. He had to try and slow down the water.

He quickly steadied his feet, swung and lifted his arm. *'Hydrolulous!'* he shouted as his arm reached its peak. The palm of his hand stood up, forbidding the water to continue but it didn't take heed. The horses looked fiercer than ever.

Determined not to give up, he swung his arm back and swept it around again before he firmly raised his palm. *'HYDROLULOUS!'* The word thundered around the walls of the square. He moved his hand out to the side. He watched, astonished, as the leading horse was forced to follow his command. It swirled around and became a normal wave. Pride swelled inside his chest, until he saw the second horse heading straight for him. It was too close to turn away.

He turned and ran, knowing that it was hopeless. He felt the first warning flurries of water swirl around his feet. He managed a feeble whistle, before he was hit in the back and winded. The water swirled around him, lifting him up. He tumbled over and over, like dirty clothes in a washing machine. Bubbles rose around him, suggesting which way was up. He struggled to swim towards the surface. His boots had filled with water and held him back.

The fight started to leave his body as he used all of his energy. *I'm going to die!* The thought terrified him.

A long thin shadow appeared above him, tempting him to try again. He pulled his knees up towards his chest and then forced his feet down below him. The push only moved him forward slightly but it was enough to grab the object. His broomstick pulled him free. The air burned his starved lungs as he gasped for breath. He struggled to hold onto his broom and hook his heel over it, slowly pulling himself on. His body sagged as he looked around to see if the others were safe. Chris was climbing onto his broom and Derek hung below his, gripping it with two hands. He couldn't see Bun anywhere. Then he spotted his broom hovering. Bun was face down in the water and wasn't making any effort to grab it.

Alfie's veins turned to ice as fear ran through them. He managed to swoop down and grab Bun's sleeve. The water turned on Alfie again. Chris and Derek flew over. They managed to flip Bun over Derek's broomstick. They didn't know if he was alive. Chris grabbed Bun's broomstick and they flew at full speed to the safety of the B&B. Alfie barely registered the dark figure watching them as the water started to subside.

*

The tale of the well had gone around the parents like wildfire. Mr and Mrs Bodley fussed around Bun, making sure that he was all right. Bun and Chris's parents arrived looking distraught.

At first they were so relieved that all the boys were safe, they smothered them in hugs and kisses.

'Alfie, Derek and Chris, go and get into some dry clothes before you freeze,' said Mrs Bodley.

They left the room but Alfie listened as the adults continued to talk.

'What were they doing?'

'I'm not sure.'

'No child should be in the Northeast Quarter in the middle of the night.'

'It's not pleasant during the day.'

'They didn't tell anyone where they were going.'

'We really have to teach them that they have to be ...'

Alfie closed the door and joined Derek and Chris upstairs, where they all changed into dry clothes.

When they came down they were told that Bun had been taken home with mild concussion.

It had been decided that a punishment was in order. It seemed odd to Alfie that because they had escaped, they needed to be punished for putting themselves in danger. He didn't think he would ever understand adults. Why weren't they just happy that everyone was safe?

CHAPTER TWENTY-ONE

The Punishment

ALFIE disliked being grounded for a week as punishment. The adults had found it hard to explain why they had given the penalty. They decided that it was for going out in the early hours of the morning without letting anyone know.

Alfie resented the fact that the barrier had blocked them. If it hadn't he and Derek would have managed to get to the well during the day and nothing would have gone wrong.

He overheard Mr and Mrs Bodley talking.

'The Highways and Byways Agency had no knowledge of the square being shut off,' said Mr Bodley.

'That's strange,' said Mrs Bodley. 'Didn't the boys say there was a sign?'

'Yes. But it wasn't supposed to be there.'

'They were still naughty not telling anyone where they were going, especially so late.'

Alfie was puzzled that the agency hadn't put the sign there. Perhaps the wrong road had been closed.

Luckily, Alfie and Derek were allowed to go and visit Bun. As they walked into his house, they were amazed that his mother was spoiling him even though he was grounded.

Bun looked up from the armchair where he was resting.

'Would you like a sweet or a drink?' he asked as he swept his hand along the huge selection.

Alfie took a sticky lolly.

'Glad to see you're managing to eat!' he joked.

'Actually I really want to get outside. I hate being stuck in here,' said Bun.

Alfie knew what he meant. The walk here had reminded him how good fresh air felt.

'I think we'd go mad if we weren't allowed out to visit you.'

'How do you feel?' asked Derek.

'Absolutely fine. Even my headache's gone,' whispered Bun, he looked around to make sure his mother hadn't overheard. 'Chris said that you managed to divert a water-horse just before we were hit.'

'Yeah, it was stunning! He turned it completely away,' said Derek.

'Gosh, Alfie, that's amazing. You must be pleased.'

Alfie enjoyed his friends' admiration, even though he was amazed that he'd managed to control water.

'The market's in town on Saturday. Alfie and I wondered if we could all meet there in the evening, if you can get away,' said Derek.

'I have to do the deliveries for Nigel but I'll hurry,' said Alfie.

Bun nodded as he grinned.

'We'll still be grounded but I'm sure we could fiddle some time to see the market. It wouldn't be for too long,' said Derek.

'Good idea,' said Bun. 'I'll tell Chris next time he visits me and we'll come up with an excuse for our parents too. I'll make sure I'm fully recovered by then.' He winked at them.

'Remember not to get better too quickly. We need the excuse to come around!' whispered Alfie as they left.

Back at the B&B, Alfie and Derek enjoyed the sun while being swallowed by the enormous chairs in the sitting room. Aunt Edith was lightly snoring.

'Did your life used to be like this before I came to stay?' Alfie shook his head. So many things had happened.

'Not at all. But then I don't go poking around like you do!'

Alfie thought for a moment. 'I think you could be onto something. Has everything happened since I overheard Damian in the Northeast Quarter?'

Derek scrunched up his face and looked at the ceiling as if he was rewinding his memory. Eventually he said, 'I can't remember.'

Alfie's memory wasn't much better. He chewed the inside of his cheek and then frowned. 'I think that water was cursed.

Otherwise it wouldn't have acted like that. It was actually aiming for us as if it intended to hurt us.' Alfie knew how ridiculous it sounded, but he kept coming back to the same conclusion.

'Who knew we were going there?' said Derek. 'It was strange. But why us?'

'None of it makes any sense unless you connect all the things together. The smoky potion and the necklace. That was a false lead. So was the well. Someone, or something, doesn't like what we're doing and is trying to get us off the trail.'

'Damian,' said Derek. 'He's the only trail we have.'

Alfie thought back to the smoky potion. 'I bet it was him outside Nigel's when the potion went smoky.'

'Yeah,' said Derek.

'He could have snuck in and added some ingredients to the cauldron to make it smoke.'

'He does have the ability,' said Derek.

Alfie nodded. He mulled over the incident at the well. 'And I'm sure I saw a figure watching us as we flew away from the well.'

'Really?'

'Yes. I was worried about Bun so I didn't really think about it seriously till now.' He squinted, trying to remember. 'I didn't see a face but it could have been Damian,' Alfie paused. 'He couldn't have found out we were on to him, could he?'

Derek just looked at him but didn't answer. Neither of them knew what to think.

*

Even though Alfie was grounded, he was still allowed to go to the potion shop as he had convinced Mrs Bodley that Nigel needed his help.

'Just make sure you come home as soon as you're finished there,' she said.

He smiled as she said *home*. He belonged in this charmed city.

'Do you think that Derek could come with me later if there are any deliveries. They're usually heavy and some of them are quite a distance.' It was worth a try as they had secretly arranged to meet Bun and Chris at the market afterwards.

Mrs Bodley looked at him. Her eyes sparkled and her smile was caring.

'If it makes it easier …'

Alfie felt guilty.

As he walked to the shop he didn't like the way he felt. Mrs Bodley was kind, even though she was strict. He knew deep down that it was so that she could protect him. Perhaps they had been stupid going to the well late at night without telling an adult, but it should have been easy. If everything had gone to plan, they would have been back and tucked up in bed without anyone knowing.

As he reached the shop he wondered if Nigel knew about the well. As soon as he entered the workshop, he learned the answer.

'Did the liquid charm come in useful?' Nigel raised both eyebrows in question as Alfie walked through the door.

'Sort of. I think I could do with a little more practice though!' Alfie lifted one side of his mouth mockingly.

'Controlling that amount of water will take years of practice, but I guess you already know that?'

Alfie nodded. 'I don't ever want to face anything like that again,' he said.

'Did you try and control it?' asked Nigel.

'Yes, I managed to get one wave to turn away from me, but there was so much water.'

'Well done! I wish I'd been there. I'm amazed how quickly you've picked everything up.' Nigel's pride made Alfie feel good. Then suddenly serious, he continued, 'But you could have been hurt.'

'I know. We were lucky.'

Alfie was pleased as Nigel relaxed.

'Pass me the third bottle from the left on the top shelf, please,' asked Nigel.

Alfie wondered what would have happened if Nigel hadn't

taught him the liquid charm, and was deep in thought as he looked around for something to stand on to help him reach the bottle.

'What are you doing?' asked Nigel, worried that Alfie wasn't using magic.

Alfie faltered, then chuckled as he willed the bottle down with the movement charm. It floated onto the bench.

'Thank you,' said Nigel. 'I thought for a moment that you'd gone off magic.' He laughed, his peace of mind restored.

'Never!' said Alfie, shaking his head. He loved the time he spent helping Nigel in the shop and workshop as much as learning the magic spells.

They made potions for all sorts of ailments. Alfie was delighted when Nigel praised his knowledge and ability. Alfie knew it was really the quality of teaching. Nigel always explained everything as he went along so that Alfie was never left wondering what he was doing. He hardly ever had to ask questions.

'Well, that's the last of that ingredient. Looks like I'll need another trip to Alice's soon.' Nigel placed the empty bottle by the door.

They were surprised to hear the city bell toll. They hadn't finished making the potions for the deliveries.

Mary popped her head around the door.

'The shop's empty. I'm going to start making supper,' she said.

Nigel looked apologetically at Alfie. 'It doesn't look like we'll have time for your lesson today,' he said.

'That's okay. I've already had enough practice this week,' Alfie responded.

The shop bell chimed and Alfie went through. He enjoyed the shop after six, when it turned into a real potion shop. It even smelled different.

Richard was shutting the door behind himself.

'I thought I'd pick up some more painkillers while I'm in this part of the city. The strength was good, but could you ask Nigel to increase it a little. I still have some left. When I start the new lot, it will need to be stronger.'

Alfie frowned and wondered what was wrong with him. It couldn't just be because he was old.

'Okay,' said Alfie. He started to go through to the workshop when Nigel came through the connecting door. Alfie thought how healthy Nigel looked compared with Richard. Surely if they'd been at school together, they'd have to be about the same age.

'Can we deliver it out to you later?' asked Nigel, 'It's been quite a busy day. I have a bit of a backlog.'

'Of course. That's fine.'

'Your illness seems to have been going on quite a while. Have you seen a doctor?' Nigel's face was filled with concern for his old friend.

'Yes,' said Richard reassuringly, 'don't worry. Hopefully I'll be as good as new soon!'

'If you're sure ...' Nigel's voice trailed off as if he didn't believe him.

As Richard turned to leave, he looked at Alfie. 'When you deliver, I'll probably still be in my shop.' He smiled as he left.

Alfie could see that Richard's suffering upset Nigel.

It took quite a while to get all the orders finished and packed. Eventually Nigel said, 'That's it. All done! You can get on with the deliveries now. I'll watch the shop.' He left through the door.

Alfie picked up the bag, looking forward to doing the deliveries with Derek.

Nigel called through from the front. 'I didn't pack Richard's. It's at the back of the bench in a potion bottle, I've run out of delivery vials.'

Alfie looked around but couldn't see it. Then he spotted it in the shadows, which made it look slightly faded. He reached out and put it in the bag.

'I'm off now. Bye!' he called out to Nigel.

He walked back to the B&B and found Derek waiting in the kitchen.

'I'll just grab a sandwich. Then we can go. Quite a few deliveries today,' said Alfie.

Mrs Bodley overheard. 'I won't expect you back too soon.'

Alfie watched Derek's face as he realised it would be a good excuse for being even later.

From the weight of the bag it was obvious that it had been a busy day for potions.

'Let me carry the bag. It's good to be out,' said Derek.

Alfie gladly passed it to him.

A lot of the customers were regulars. Alfie knew the way to their houses without thinking. He enjoyed delivering to new customers, discovering streets he hadn't been down before.

'I didn't know that there were so many little passageways. We can hardly fit down this one.' Derek started to laugh. 'Imagine if Mr Locksley tried!'

Alfie was shocked. Then he started to laugh too.

'The path would be closed until he'd starved himself thin.'

'They'd have to remove his knitting needles, though.' Derek laughed again. Alfie had told Derek about the knitted cakes.

The smell alerted Alfie that they'd arrived in the Northeast Quarter. It was sour, as if he'd stuck a mouldy lemon up his nose. He would never get used to it. Shivers ran up and down his spine, which were made worse by the memory of the well. They eventually came to Richard's shop.

Looking along the street, Alfie realised what a narrow escape he'd had when he'd crashed on his broom. The area was tiny. Large glass windows lined the street. The thought of hitting them at speed made him feel sick. He was grateful for the thick layer of dirt that covered the cobbles and made the landing softer. Without it, it would have been like dropping from the sky onto a pebbly beach.

Alfie used his shoulder to open the door to Richard's shop. The bell jangled violently. As Richard was huddled with some customers, Alfie stood for a minute wondering what to do. Richard seemed too busy to greet him.

Alfie decided that Nigel wouldn't mind if he didn't collect the money. Richard could pay next time he was in the shop. He took the bottle out of the bag and held it up so that Richard could see him. Richard nodded. Alfie put the bottle down on a small table by the door. When Richard nodded again, Alfie left the shop.

'That was the last one. We'll go back past the market. We've been quick with the deliveries so Mrs Bodley won't expect us for ages,' said Alfie.

Derek looked pleased. 'I love the market. There's so much to see. Now that it's after six, you'll see all the old magic. It's quite different. I think a lot of it has been forgotten.' Derek seemed to love the older ways of practising magic.

When they were about halfway back, the street opened up into a small bustling square. Tables and chairs were filled with people enjoying the freedom of the evening. Contented sounds mingled together as they laughed and chatted.

Alfie looked around at the smiling faces. His gaze was drawn to the tree in the centre of the square. Its gnarled trunk showed its age. It twisted up and split into branches that carried the most amazing leaves. They glowed in the moonlight, lighting the square. *Why haven't I noticed that tree before?* he wondered.

'I've never seen anything like that,' he said, and nodded towards the tree.

'It's a moon tree. It's good that you've seen it at night. During the day it's pretty ordinary.'

'I've been here during the day and never even noticed it. It looks magical at night.'

'I don't think it's magic,' said Derek. 'Come on, let's get to the market so we can spend longer there.' His excitement was contagious. Alfie ran to catch him up. He wondered what the market was going to be like.

The old-fashioned scene immediately enchanted Alfie. Colours, sounds and smells hit his senses. The gowns and cloaks worn by everyone glowed golden in the moonlight. The stalls were made of wood, their intricate carvings worn smooth from centuries of use. The roofs were held high by ornate posts, their fabric flapped softly in the evening breeze. He watched from the edge as people moved between the stalls.

Soft, haunting music drifted through the air. He looked for the source of it and spotted a peculiar accordion with huge, leather bellows, one at each end, that gasped in air before blowing it out. It stood alone, puffing away under its own steam. The lullaby was strangely calming.

Some stalls were packed with food, mountains of delicious homemade cakes, snacks and sweets. The glorious smells made Alfie's stomach rumble. He moved into the hustle and bustle of the bazaar and bought the stickiest chocolate biscuit he had ever seen. His first bite confirmed that it was also the tastiest, the intensity of the chocolate almost burst his taste buds. His tongue reached out to capture the last bits that ran down his chin.

Alfie and Derek walked through the market. Stallholders bellowed, approaching passers-by with items that they encouraged them to buy. The list was endless; books, food, clothes, and bolts of fabric in every colour imaginable. Some were so unusual! He'd never seen anything like it before.

At a jewellery stall Alfie saw a Big Ben pocket watch.

'Always shows the correct time, that one does,' said the stallholder. 'Or, how about this long distance monocle. It closes the gap and brings far away sights closer.'

Alfie took it, rested it on his cheek and perched his eyebrow over the top.

'You look like an old man.' Derek laughed as Alfie tried to keep the monocle in place.

He closed his other eye and looked through the monocle towards a wizard in the distance. He could see every thread of his cloak. He caught it as it popped away from his eye and put it down next to some spectacles. A sign beside them said: *Sample specs. Will that new paint colour suit your room? Glance through them to see it newly painted.*

The stallholder wasn't going to give up easily. 'Try this old camera. Take a photograph now and the picture will show you at any age you want!'

Alfie didn't notice Chris and Bun approaching as he left Derek behind. He headed towards a bookstall. He needed all the help he could get to outwit Damian. He felt sure time was running out. Perhaps amongst all the books about dragons and unicorns or potions and antiques, there would be some clue tucked away that would help him.

He frowned as he walked over. The pile of books was enormous. He wondered whether to waste his time looking. He started to turn away when a book caught his eye, *Ancient Magical Objects*. His hand reached out of its own volition and picked up the book. It was heavy. The leather cover felt dry and ready to peel off in big, dead flakes. A shiver of dislike ran down his spine. Even though he didn't think books carried diseases he didn't want to hold it. He rested it on some other books while he flicked through. A musty smell floated from the pages. They showed objects of all shapes and sizes, claiming to contain anything from luck to genies. He turned the pages quickly until it dawned on him that the blue necklace might be in there. His lips thinned when he didn't find it.

What else could harm Nigel? He flicked through again slowly, eager to see if something stood out. He started to read the descriptions, hoping that they would steer him in the right direction, but nothing jumped out at him. Disappointed, he wondered if the author had made up all the items in it.

He shut the book and half-threw it back to its original place. *Stupid book,* he thought as it landed. It opened on a page that he hadn't seen. The picture was the same as the Orb he'd seen in Richard's shop. There was no mistaking it. Big, bold letters named it the Death Orb. The inscription below said: *For the lucky ones, it causes instant death when touched…*

Alfie frowned as he questioned the word "lucky" but he read on …*but the unlucky ones, who touch it through another live entity, will have a prolonged and painful death.*

Alfie stood completely still. *Richard has the Orb.* His mind started whirring. Richard's dog had dropped down dead in the park. Now Richard was in constant pain. He must have been stroking his dog when it had picked up the Orb. He was dying in pain – very slowly.

That was why he constantly needed painkillers. Alfie moved forward to grab the book but jolted the table. The unstable pile of books tumbled to the floor like a waterfall. The stallholder shouted. Alfie shook his head and mouthed *Sorry*. He didn't have time to help pick them up.

He stepped back from the stall in shock. His lungs felt small – breathing hurt. One thought wound its way to the front of his mind, *This Orb must have been the one that Mervyn had used to try to kill Martyn. Poor Richard…*

He needed to find Derek. He turned sharply, ready to run but he bumped into Nigel.

'I thought it was you,' said Nigel. 'Are you alright?'

Alfie looked up at him.

'I – I was just thinking.' He didn't know how to tell Nigel about Richard.

'You seem to be having a bad day. When I went back into the workshop, I saw that you'd left Richard's medicine behind.'

Alfie was confused.

'But I took it to him.'

'No, this is it.' Nigel handed him a bottle.

Alfie took it but was still confused.

Nigel tried to explain. 'The bottle you took had nothing in it. Well nothing important anyway. I only keep it for sentimental reasons.'

Alfie remembered that the bottle he had delivered looked slightly faded.

'What do you mean?' he asked slowly.

Nigel looked embarrassed. 'It's rather silly, really. When I was young, Richard knew that I wanted to be a potion maker so he bought me my first bottle – that's where the blue comes from.' He smiled at the memory. 'I keep an old scrap of parchment from our childhood in that bottle.'

Alfie's skin felt clammy. His jaw went limp as he tilted his head.

Nigel kept talking. 'Richard was very ill when we were younger. I was at his house trying to cheer him up.' Nigel smiled again.

'Anyway, because he was my best friend, I drew up a contract saying that I would die instead of him. I signed it but he refused, saying that I was too good a friend ... he didn't want me to die.' His chin wrinkled. 'See, I said it was silly...'

Alfie froze as he remembered what he'd overheard in the Northeast Quarter: *It's far more significant than he thinks...*

Some of the bits slotted into place. He began to feel sick with fear.

'What was the contract written on?'

Nigel looked puzzled at the odd question. 'Just some old parchment that I had found in his father's study.'

Alfie remembered that Richard's father had been a lawyer.

'What was it like? Heavy and golden?' he asked warily.

'Yes,' said Nigel, and then as an afterthought, 'it was probably rather expensive but I didn't use much.'

Binding Parchment! Alfie turned and ran to find Derek.

He could hear Nigel shout after him. 'Don't worry. It's not official. He never signed it!' He was laughing. He really didn't realise the importance of it.

But he can sign it now that he has the piece of parchment! He ran through the market stalls like a thief being chased. He gasped for breath, desperate to find Derek. He couldn't get the contract back on his own. He almost collapsed with relief when he spotted him.

'It's Richard who wants to kill Nigel. Not Damian! We have to go to Richard's shop. He has a contract stating that Nigel will die instead of him.'

Derek held out his hands and frowned. It didn't make sense.

'Richard is dying from a horrible curse,' shouted Alfie.

Derek looked horrified.

'I know it sounds impossible, but I found this really old book and it proved it. Honestly, this is real this time.' Alfie had to make Derek believe him.

'If that's true, do you really think he'll let us have the contract back?' asked Derek.

Alfie felt a thump in his chest as he remembered how desperately

Richard had fought to keep Nigel safe from the falling building. He couldn't let him die. He needed him alive so that he could take Nigel's life as his own.

'No,' he said. 'I don't think he's going to let us have it back.'

Derek understood.

'I'll go and find Bun and Chris. They're around here somewhere.'

Alfie felt as if he was treading quicksand. His thoughts refused to fit together. Every time they almost did, something niggled so that they sprung apart again. He tried to force them to fuse, but they were going round and round in a circle.

When Derek returned with the other two, Alfie hadn't moved.

Suddenly the pieces fitted together. Alfie could see all of the events that had taken place since he'd arrived in Wyckerton.

He spoke as if he was replaying a film, 'None of this has been Damian. We've been chasing the wrong person. He had nothing to do with the smoky potion or the well. Richard is dying. When Nigel was young, he wrote a contract offering his life to Richard and he wrote it on *Binding Parchment!* That's what Richard's been looking for. I've just delivered it because it was in a potion bottle.'

Bun and Chris looked horrified. 'Dregs,' they said in unison.

'I told Richard that someone was trying to kill Nigel…'

'I remember. You said you had told him when you crashed your broom,' interrupted Bun.

Alfie carried on, '…so he tried to put us off the trail with the smoky potion and the blue necklace.'

'Then it was Richard outside Nigel's shop when the potion went smoky?' Derek frowned.

Alfie nodded. 'Mr Locksley was supposed to leave that evening. We would never have known that the necklace wasn't the right object. Mr Locksley bought it from Richard's shop. I know he told him he was leaving for Ireland. It would have worked if the train hadn't been cancelled. Richard probably thought we'd give up.'

'And you would never have found out that it could be broken. Only Nigel was supposed to be able to do that,' said Derek. 'When I showed Richard the broken necklace, he seemed disappointed.

At the time I thought he felt sorry for us, but it was because he knew we would keep searching.'

'We also bumped into him when I received the letter that made us go to the well. As we flew away from the well, I saw a figure. Derek and I thought it was Damian, but now I know it was Richard. He decided to get rid of us to stop us interfering.' Alfie found the idea sickening.

Bun was indignant. 'But I almost died!'

'I *think* that was the point,' said Derek.

'We all felt sorry for Richard – and he was doing this to us,' whispered Chris.

All four of them stood there, too stunned to speak.

Alfie remembered something else.

'As well as Damian, Richard was close to Nigel's shop when he was burgled. I'd forgotten that. I thought Damian was to blame,' he looked at Derek, who nodded to confirm it. 'Everything had been disturbed except the potion bottles. Richard needed painkillers. He couldn't destroy his supply.' Alfie felt weak as the explanation became clear.

'Good grief!' said Derek in disbelief.

'I don't understand why Richard saved Nigel from that building, though.' Chris looked confused.

'The contract stated that Nigel would die for him. He needed to accept it by signing it. If Nigel had been killed by the falling building, Richard wouldn't have been able to take over his life.'

'That's awful…' said Chris.

'Hopefully he doesn't know that he has the contract.' Alfie had just left the bottle because Richard had been busy. 'Come on. We have to get over there. Quick.'

They started to run.

'How will we get the contract back?' asked Bun.

'We'll have to break into the shop.' Alfie knew it would be the only way. 'Now! Before he finds out that he has the contract! Richard had other painkillers to use up first. Hopefully he hasn't looked at the new bottle yet.'

No one said anything as they ran. All too scared now that they knew what they were dealing with.

Alfie hoped the moonlight would mask them in the dark streets of the Northeast Quarter. They ran quickly and soon left the pleasant streets for narrower lanes that confirmed where they were heading.

Alfie tried not to think of what was ahead. He knew deep down that he wasn't just going to walk into Richard's shop and pick up the bottle, but he pretended to himself that he might.

Derek's voice quivered, 'I can't believe we're doing this.'

Alfie looked at him sharply. 'If you don't like it, go back!'

'Don't be like that. I don't like it, but it needs to be done,' said Derek.

Alfie felt bad for shouting. 'I know. We'll be fine once we're there.'

As they got closer they started to walk. The lanes became dingy, dark alleyways. Alfie scrunched up his nose to keep out the revolting smells. His neck hairs stood up as they walked along. A few lone figures were hanging around. Some were moving along the alleyway going about their business. Others were tucked into doorways and half-hidden, staring, making him feel wary and scared.

The alleyway led to a wider street. Alfie held up his hand and stopped.

'It's at the end of this row.' He pointed at the shop. They all sank into the shadows.

Alfie moved so that he could see the shop. He felt his stomach churn. No light glowed through the glass. Even the rooms above were in darkness.

He wished that he'd just shaken the bottle and realised there was no liquid in it.

'Wait here,' he whispered, and moved off quietly.

He flattened his body against the wall next door and rolled sideways to look through the window. He moved his head forward and tried to focus through the murky darkness. Even when he squinted, he couldn't see much. He looked down at the window display. Not much on show. He crept back to the others.

'The door sticks, remember?' he whispered, and looked at Derek.

'I'd forgotten that. How will we get in without making a noise?'

'The window locks look pretty flimsy. There's not much stuff on the sill. It's very dark inside. I'm not sure if the bottle is where I left it.'

'Once we're in, we'll find it.' Derek seemed to be used to the idea of breaking in now.

'You're all still okay with this?' Alfie didn't want to pressure anyone.

The other three spoke in unison, 'Yes!'

'Okay. Two of us need to keep watch out here. One should guard the door at the back, in case Richard comes through.' They nodded. 'I'll find the bottle.'

'I'll come in and watch the back door,' offered Derek.

'Let's do it!' Alfie's stomach muscles clenched making him feel sick but he swung around and headed for the shop.

Chris walked to the far side of the shop and looked around. He nodded back to them that it was clear. Bun raised one hand to magically unlatch the lock on the window and then used both hands to silently draw it open. Derek went through the opening first and waited inside.

Alfie's legs felt like jelly. He could hardly stand, let alone climb through the window. He looked around at the others, then shook his head to get control of himself, ready to climb in. He sat on the windowsill and twisted to swing his feet around, then lowered them, and almost hit a table full of vases. He froze. Derek and Bun both raised their hands ready to magically catch anything that fell. Alfie felt a nervous laugh rising inside. Derek gritted his teeth and opened his eyes wide, willing him not to laugh. Alfie moved again. He lowered his feet to the floor with a tiny thud and stood up unsteadily.

'Who's there?' The question hung in the air.

Alfie didn't know what to do. He looked at Derek who was frozen to the spot. A match strike sounded before Richard's face was lit from below. His features appeared sunken. He moved into shadow as he lifted the match to light an oil lamp. He was sitting at his desk and picked up the unopened potion bottle.

'What on earth are you doing?' Richard almost growled in disbelief.

Alfie tried to think fast.

'Um – I delivered the wrong bottle. I have your medication here.' He put his hand into his pocket and felt the bottle that Nigel had given him at the market. He breathed a sigh of relief as he removed his hand and held up the bottle, realising that it just might work.

A slow, wide smile appeared on Richard's face. 'This isn't the wrong bottle. Though it might turn out to be for Nigel. I should have realised he'd hide the contract in a potion bottle.' With the light from the lamp shining through the blue glass, the paper inside the bottle was clearly visible. Richard popped the cork lid out and tried to push his finger in to withdraw the piece of parchment.

Alfie moved towards him and Richard stood up.

'How could you plan to kill your best friend?' said Alfie. He stopped walking.

'He's not my friend. I have much darker ones!' Richard's grip tightened on the bottle, turning his knuckles white. 'This,' he held up the bottle, 'will enable me to continue serving the darkest of them all.' He scowled.

Alfie glared at him.

'You amused me at first but then you couldn't stop interfering,' revealed Richard.

'Is that why you tricked us into going to the well?'

'Yes. I needed you to receive that letter. I addressed it to you and made your name disappear once you'd opened it. That way, you stupid boy, you'd think it was just a leaflet and not realise someone was tricking you. I needed you to come back at night when no one else was around, that's why I boarded it up. I knew your loyalty to your friends and your inquisitive mind would bring you back as soon as the board was gone.'

'It was you we saw there. It wasn't even a proper wishing well, was it?' Alfie hated the fact that they'd been tricked.

Richard sneered at him.

'But we could have died!'

'You were becoming a nuisance,' exclaimed Richard, 'always trying to protect Nigel.'

'But he's helped you to cope with your pain.'

'Yes, I liked that. He was keeping me strong while I looked for the contract. I knew he wouldn't have destroyed it. He's far too sentimental.' Richard's face showed his dislike of Nigel's friendship.

Alfie felt a flash of anger rip through him and he stepped forward.

'I wouldn't do that if I were you,' said Richard, standing as tall as possible.

Alfie saw real evil in Richard's twisted face.

But I have to save Nigel. He continued moving towards Richard.

'I said STOP!' Spittle left Richard's mouth like venom. His arm came up as he spoke.

Alfie felt a thump in his chest as he was lifted up and thrown across the room. His back slammed into the wall and he slid down to the floor, fighting for breath. He could only watch as Derek attempted a spell but was magically lifted up towards the ceiling by Richard's outstretched arm. Richard glowered as he suspended Derek, before he dragged his arm backwards. Derek fell straight down, hitting his head as he crashed to the floor. His body flopped over, as he lay unconscious.

Bun and Chris came in through the window and advanced on Richard. He challenged them but they continued to approach him, ignoring his warning.

Both of them were hurled back towards the window with one sweep of Richard's arm.

Alfie looked back toward Richard as he sat down. Now desperate, he tipped the contract out of the potion bottle. He carefully unrolled it and laid it on the desk in front of him. His signature would seal the deal with Nigel.

'*Momentum,*' shouted Bun. Unnoticed, he had crawled closer to Richard. The parchment flew off the desk and onto the floor.

Richard pushed with two hands on his desk, stood up and moved towards the parchment. Alfie grabbed the edge of a table and pulled himself up with one hand, the other in front of him, clutching his stomach. He flicked his hand and shouted, '*Momentum!*' A lamp flew across the room towards Richard. Chris and Bun joined in, magically hurling every antique they could towards him. Old lamps, china cups, teapots and ornaments flew at Richard from all directions.

He scowled at them as he deflected each item. 'How dare you think that you can use your childish magic on me!' He raised his arm and flung all three boys across the room, slamming Alfie and Bun into the wall. Alfie gasped in horror as he watched Chris smash through the huge glass window at the front of the shop.

The effort of the fight was taking its toll on Richard. He picked up the parchment and moved back to his desk. As he sat down, his body sagged.

Alfie felt hopeless. Richard was too powerful. He had controlled the water from the well and Alfie hadn't stood a chance against it. He watched Richard through the glass of the tall cabinet as he picked up a quill. *It can't end like this.* He frantically looked around for something to help him defeat Richard. Chris started to climb back through the window, covered in specks of blood.

Richard lifted his head, his eyes burning into Alfie. He sneered as he moved the quill towards the inkwell, getting ready to sign the contract and take Nigel's life as his own.

As Richard moved, a tiny diamond in his ring reflected a line of light across the room. It hit the cabinet and lit up the Death Orb into a kaleidoscope of colours.

Alfie gasped. His chest hurt as he focussed on the Orb. He raised his hand, palm up. '*Momentum!*' he whispered. Nigel's face flashed through his mind.

He flicked his wrist. The hovering Orb smashed through the glass of the cabinet and flew towards Richard.

Everything became slow motion as Alfie watched the Orb fly through the air.

Richard dropped the quill and raised his hand, ready to catch the weapon flying towards him.

Please don't guess what it is. Alfie held his breath, determined not to warn Richard what was flying towards him.

The Orb made direct contact with the palm of Richard's hand. His hand jerked as horror crossed his face. He knew what he had touched. The Orb dropped onto the desk in front of him, knocking over the inkwell.

Richard's mouth opened, but nothing came out. He focused on them as they stood together. His last thought must have been that four children had defeated him. His body crumbled to the ground.

Alfie moved closer, scared that Richard would stand up again.

The others joined him. They watched as the pain left Richard's face, revealing that he was dead.

The Binding Parchment soaked up the spilt ink but the words remained untouched as the paper turned blue.

CHAPTER TWENTY-TWO

Victory

THEY arrived back at Nigel's shop in record time. Alfie banged on the locked shop door until Nigel came and opened it.

'We managed to get the contract back!' Alfie held it out.

Nigel frowned. He didn't know what Alfie was talking about. 'What contract?'

Alfie realised that Nigel didn't even know they had gone back to Richard's.

'The one in the potion bottle that I delivered to Richard earlier.'

Nigel took the ink-stained parchment and looked at Alfie in disbelief.

Alfie wished he didn't have to explain. He knew that Nigel would be upset by how evil Richard had become. 'It wasn't Damian who wanted to … to … kill you,' Alfie found it difficult to say kill, 'it was Richard. He was dying slowly from the Death Orb and he wanted to use your life so he could stay alive.'

Alfie explained everything.

'But this is Binding Parchment, if he had signed it…' Nigel slowly sat down on the shop steps, suddenly aware of the seriousness of what he was holding.

Alfie's chest rose as he breathed in deeply, happy that they'd succeeded.

'It's all over now.' Alfie wanted to reassure him.

'I wouldn't have realised when I took this parchment from his father's office…' Nigel was still shocked.

'And I wouldn't have known what it was if I hadn't gone to the law firm with Aunt Edith,' said Alfie.

'I've kept it all this time.' Nigel shook his head, unable to believe the events. He started to rip the parchment into tiny pieces.

'I'm afraid that Richard is dead.' Alfie felt sad that Nigel's friend had ended up so evil.

'But thanks to all of you, it wasn't me!' Nigel looked at them and smiled. 'I'm sorry I didn't believe you,' he said as his gaze reached Alfie.

Alfie felt his heart swell. He was lucky to know Nigel.

'You've helped me so much. It was good to do something for you.' Alfie was glad that he hadn't given up.

Nigel took a deep breath and stood up, eventually noticing Chris's cuts and Derek's bruises.

'Goodness me. Let's get those sorted,' he said, and walked back into the shop.

With Nigel's creams and potions, Derek and Chris were soon feeling better.

'Why don't we see if Mary has enough cake for everyone?' said Nigel.

'We'd better get back actually. We're all still grounded!' Alfie suddenly remembered.

'Not for long!' laughed Nigel, and he shouted up to Mary, 'Come down here, please. We're going to have a party!'

As Nigel led them around to the B&B, everyone talked at once. Alfie stopped and watched them all walk ahead. He shut his eyes. *It could have been so different from this.* He was grateful that it had worked out well.

Both Bun and Chris's parents soon arrived at the B&B after hearing the news.

Alfie explained everything: the smoky potion, the necklace and the wishing well.

Mr Bodley shook his head. 'How did you find out that it was Richard?'

'I found a book at the market.' Alfie looked at Mrs Bodley. She smiled, not minding that it had been when he was grounded. 'It explained about the Death Orb. I'd seen it at Richard's shop. When Nigel told me about the contract that he had written when he was a boy, it made sense.'

'Why did you write a contract like that?' Mr Bodley looked at Nigel.

Nigel looked sheepish. 'Richard was so ill. We were best friends and I wanted to cheer him up. I didn't know what Binding Parchment was back then and I've never really thought about it since.' Nigel shook his head. 'I didn't realise how dangerous that contract was or I would never have kept it.'

The adults listened in awe. All four boys were hailed as true heroes. They didn't have to worry about being grounded anymore.

Chris and Bun's fathers disappeared with Mr Bodley and Nigel. They returned later in a triumphant state.

When Alfie could get a word in, he asked, 'What happened?'

Mr Bodley was almost dancing. 'We shattered the Death Orb,' he said.

'It sounds impressive,' admitted Nigel, 'but even though it was very powerful it was quite delicate.'

'It was fantastic when it exploded into a million pieces.' Mr Bodley was still excited.

Alfie smiled. Thankfully, no one would ever suffer from its curse again.

*

Alfie settled back into normal life quickly. He helped in Nigel's workshop but something kept coming back to haunt him.

Eventually he had to ask, 'When we were at Richard's shop he said he had very dark friends. Do you think he meant Mervyn?' Alfie tried to sound casual as he watched Nigel, gauging his reaction.

At first Nigel stood completely still. Then he slowly turned towards Alfie and smiled.

'It's very unlikely. But according to the legend, I suppose it could be possible, if he *was* entombed somewhere. I think it's more likely to be the dark friends that Richard had made.'

Alfie nodded, unsure whether Nigel's answer made him feel any better.

*

Many of the residents of Wyckerton greeted Alfie warmly as he did the deliveries. Alfie avoided the Northeast Quarter, as it still made him feel uncomfortable, even though he had dealt with the evil that dwelt there. It was secretive … as if it was biding its time.

*

No non-magics at school knew what had happened, of course. Lessons carried on as usual. The teachers warned them of the approaching exams.

Alfie received a letter from his father informing him that he would be coming back for a few weeks during the summer holidays. For a moment Alfie panicked. Would his father want to stay at the B&B?

When he mentioned it to Mrs Bodley, she reassured him. 'Don't fret, the charm will deal with it.'

Alfie wondered how the charm would sort it out.

*

By the time the exams came around, Alfie's new confidence helped him cope. He knew he hadn't done outstandingly well in any subject but was pleased that he had succeeded in equally important things that year, including defeating an evil wizard.

On the Saturday afternoon of the parents' meeting, Alfie and Derek nervously waited to find out what the teachers had said. Alfie had been working at Nigel's all day but was waiting to see his school report before doing the deliveries.

'My parents are taking ages,' said Derek. 'And I'm starving.' He popped two pieces of bread into the toaster.

The smell of freshly toasted bread made Alfie's mouth water. As Derek spread the butter, Alfie watched it melt. He jumped up, put two more pieces of bread in the machine and fiddled with the dial before he sat down again.

He sat and worried about what the Bodley's would say when they returned. 'I'm dreading my report,' he said, and twiddled his thumbs. The burning smell made him jump up. 'Oh no! It's burnt.'

'How badly?'

'Loads. What does it matter?'

'Just wondered if it needed minus one or two,' said Derek, getting up.

Alfie screwed up his face.

'To un-burn it,' said Derek as he put the toast back in the toaster and adjusted the dial to minus two. Within a minute the toaster pushed up perfectly browned toast.

Alfie couldn't help grinning as he buttered the golden bread.

He sat down at the table. He nibbled the toast and wondered if he'd made the right decision about coming back to the B&B before doing the deliveries.

The noise from the entrance hall told him that it was too late to change his mind. Mr and Mrs Bodley had arrived back from the school. They were talking rather loudly, indicating that it hadn't gone well. Alfie and Derek decided to hide but didn't manage to leave the kitchen before the adults came in.

'I really don't think it's very funny, Peter,' said Mrs Bodley crossly.

'Sorry, but I couldn't help it,' he replied as he spotted the two boys.

Derek found his voice first, 'How did it go?' he asked.

'Very well, apart from your father!' said Mrs Bodley, glaring at Mr Bodley. 'He asked every teacher that we saw why the meeting couldn't be held in the evening, so that he could hear their excuses.'

Mr Bodley winked at them. Alfie was pleased when he realised that it was Mr Bodley who was in trouble and not them.

'They all think they make the decisions,' Mr Bodley said, smiling.

'Anyway,' said Mrs Bodley, not wanting to get into another argument. 'You've both done well. Science marks are good. The English teacher said that he was pleased with your progress, Alfie, particularly your note-taking.' She looked puzzled. 'I don't really understand why you take notes in English. Shouldn't you be writing essays?' She looked at both of them but they just shrugged.

Alfie wondered for a moment if Mr Kalm was aware that they constantly passed notes during his lessons but dismissed the idea. He had never told them off.

'Neither of you are trying hard enough in geography. She seemed such a caring teacher...' said Mrs Bodley.

'Pah,' said Mr Bodley, but turned it into a cough when Mrs Bodley glared at him again.

Caring wasn't a word Alfie could associate with Mrs Stott. He was relieved that Mr Bodley had summed her up correctly. *Why had Mrs Bodley been hoodwinked?* wondered Alfie.

'And maths, well, the maths teacher was very disappointed in the untidiness of your work.' She frowned at both of them. 'I don't think she actually mentioned the quality, though...'

That's about right. Miss Lloyd was more obsessed with tidiness than she was with correct answers.

'But overall it seems that you're both getting along fine,' said Mr Bodley as he walked towards them. 'I need a cup of tea and a cake. Care to join me, dear...' He glanced at Alfie and jutted his head toward the door, unseen by Mrs Bodley.

They both fled unscathed, thanks to Mr Bodley aiding their escape.

*

About a week later another letter arrived from his father.

Dearest Alfie,

It seems such a silly idea for me to come back to Wyckerton, when there is so much I want to show you here, in China. I know that you will love it.

I am enclosing an air ticket so that you can join me for the summer.

Love as always, Dad x

Alfie looked forward to exploring. He was quite content that magic would wait until he returned to Wyckerton at the end of the summer holiday.